CHIMERA'S LAY

SCHOOL DAYS

Kiltron

Copyright © 2021 by Dan Harrington

All rights reserved.

No part of this publication may be produced, distributed, or transmitted in any form or by any means, including photocopying, recording, or other electronic or mechanical methods, without the prior written permission of the author, except in the case of brief quotations embodied in critical reviews and certain other non-commercial uses permitted by copyright law.

ISBN
(Paperback) 9798508030681
ASIN
(eBook) B095ND5JWZ

I dedicate this book to all the Anime fans out there who have had to deal with the shitty protagonists of harem stories.
This is for you!

Praise

I like to praise **Jay Crudge** for a lot of ideas he has thrown at me over the years. Had some good times brother with our insults back and forth. It brought us great joy making fun of the world and all the stupid shit out there.

Now, this story is an idea that just sort of came out of nowhere for me. Damn, straight this is a sexual power fantasy, baby! Not going to try to hide it. I will write what the hell I want.

Want to thank **Derek Fehr** and his wife **Melissa Fehr** for their support of my work. "Hey man, just write what you like," Derek said adamantly. They buy every copy that is published. Signed and personalized! Stop reading my shit to your son. They are not bedtime stories, Yoh! Lol!

Warning

For all you, triggers out there. Reader discretion is advised. This shit will offend you. It makes fun of dumb fucktards and is dark as fuck and I don't pull punches. There are hijinks and sex galore. Sometimes scenes of rape, but mostly of men. Hey women like to be rough too. There are also reverse harems in here too. Can't let men have all the fun. So, Cum on in and play. Guarantee you will have a good old time here in Chimera's Lane.

May the deep peace of the running wave be with you!

"Kiltron has built up a lore and world of dark crazy hijinks.
The protagonist is a character you can relate to and care about.
At last, a harem story done right!"
-Jay Crudge

"This just proves the madness that resides in Kiltron's mind.
Dark, gritty, passionate!
Only he could come up with such bizarre insanity!"
-Various Methods

"As to be expected, he writes off the wall stories that grip you and never let go.
Just a marvel how his mind works!"
-Derek Fehr

"Splendid storytelling!
His wacky mind never disappoints!
-Melissa Fehr

A small insight to the world of Glen and his gang bang friends!

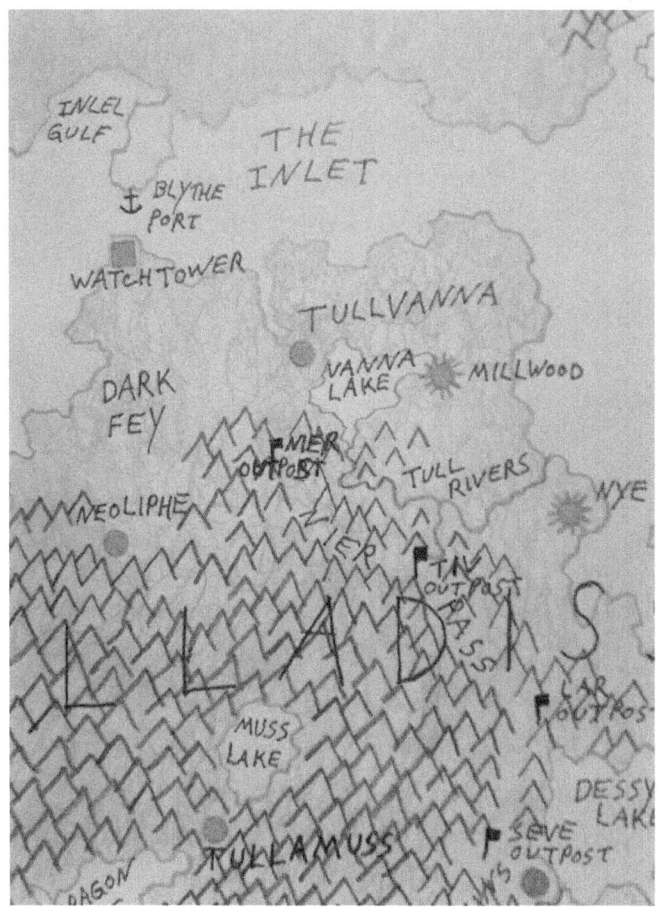

Tullvanna is where the school is!

A Bit of History

Ruination of war;
Only corrupts the heart.
Sour, are the souls;
That want to dominate!
-*Chimera's Lay*

War ravaged the world for over a thousand years. Not only were the humans fighting each other but were slaughtering the other races as well.

There seemed to be no end in sight as armies marched across nations. Blood stained the lands and flowed in the rivers. Forests were burned to cinders to drive monster kind out of their homes. The human nations sometime even had temporary alliances so, that these foul creatures could be exterminated. As with humans these alliances would never last as they too, would betray one another to gain power.

The elves helped to rally monster kind to drive the humans back and for a time that worked. The elves had their own problems of strife within the ranks. The Aeryn-Soon Elves were the largest and most powerful elven nation and they too thought themselves above all others.

Nations fell into civil strife. Revolutions fractured kingdoms in two. Hunts for rare monsters to claim their magic. Anyone and everyone that was different, destroyed. The world became brutalized in blood and gore. Rape and pillage of ever race and culture. It was mass genocide.

Then the dragons came with cleansing fire. They went to every nation to parley a deal to stop the bloodshed. Those that defied the dragons, were burned. In no time all kingdoms and races complied. No one had the power to go against the dragons. Not even the Angels or Demons had that kind of power. As proof they too had to comply with the rules that were set.

All citizens of the world whether they be human, demi-human (their kind were considered a grave sin and abominations), Monster kind, elves, fae, faerie, demons, angels, lizard kin, serpent kind, and all the underwater kingdoms included. Not even the seas could save anyone from a dragon's flame. They were godlike creatures in the world of Drayvonn.

So, as it were everyone had twenty-five years to rebuild clean up their act, and to send their heir apparent to the kingdom of Tulladiss for schooling. This would be the first school for the children of the new era to learn, together.

This would be an opportunity to rid themselves of old prejudices and hatreds. This generation was a new hope for a better world. Change was needed. Change was on the horizon more than anyone could ever know.

Let the decree of the dragons be known!

Observing

Grades are important;
But so are your social skills!
-Professor Taka

A procession of young students made their way along the streets of Tullvanna to the main building of the school. Today was to be a lecture on the rules and regulations.

Thus far a girl and her younger sister were on a rooftop watching all the passerby's walk to their destinations. They wanted to observe everyone and find out who was who before hand. Some people they have managed to find out their identities. Others were not worth the time of day. Besides, it was the students of the main houses that mattered. Still, no one seemed interesting enough to take notice of.

"Hey sis, look. That's Trevor from The Dhyme. He is so handsome," the younger sister said as she leaned on the rail of the widow's walk. She gave a long sigh.

Violet gave a sideways glance at her sister. Her strawberry-coloured hair was tied in pigtails. The blonde highlights made her hair more orange like than anything. She was a petite girl with barely had any curves at all and she wore scantly clad clothing to show off what she did not have. Although, she had a bubble butt. She was fifteen summers. She still had growing to do.

Poppy's hazel eyes turned a deep blue as she looked upon Trevor. She licked her lips, then pierced them.

Violet smiled knowingly. The older sister glanced to the young lord of The Dhyme kingdom. He was large and muscled. In Violet's mind he was all bronze and no brains. His hair was longer than most women's as it's straights strains brew in the breeze. His hair was so pale yellow it almost looked white. He wore the furs of his nation. He waved to the crowd as he walked by. They seemed to like him thus far.

Violet continued to pretend to be disinterested in the people from the other kingdoms. There were so many that could not be seen as they sat in carriages to hide themselves.

After a while less and less people were going to the school. Violet was about to tell her sister it was time to go when people started to cheer.

"Look, Violet," she screeched excitedly and pointed. Violet looked in the direction her sister pointed to. The procession came down the street. An odd-looking carriage was being drawn by large drakes.

Violet knew who was in that carriage. It was Princess Catrice of Tulladiss. She was part of the ruling cast here in this kingdom. Her family had a part to play in setting up this school system. Then there was her guardian who rode along side the carriage. She looked very capable. Her auburn hair had many braids interweaved together into a single long braid that hung down past her hips.

Then Violet saw something unbelievable and her eyes widened. It did not go unnoticed by her sister Poppy. The girl smiled and watched as Violet's mouth was slightly agape. The man who rode behind the carriage was taller than most men. He was muscular in build and sculpted to perfection. He had extremely long black hair so dark that it looked like it absorbed the very sunlight shinning on it. Full kissable lips. His skin was golden and molten like. There was no one in the world that had such skin. Then there were his eyes. Eyes unlike anything possible in this world. They were silver, bright, and shiny like the very metal.

Violet's own eyes went fully the colour of her name's sake. Her magic brewed within her. It rolled and squirmed like a beast in heat.

Then she noted the hooded figure riding beside him. They were looking right at her. Violet was taken back to being seen. Violet eyed the rider. She suspected they were a woman by the small delicate hands holding the reins. She had to watch that one. There was something foreboding about the cloaked figure. Violet shivered involuntarily.

Violet was left to her thoughts. When she had a harem of her own, that man would be the perfect trophy to display in her bed. His exoticness excited her. She had never desired anything before. She just took what she wanted. This was different. It was a yearning she felt would grow out of control some day.

She looked to her sister.

"Poppy! Let's go," Violet spoke softly.

Poppy nodded and the two girls left the roof top. It was time for their first day of school.

First Day of School?

> Observing is a precious skill!
> -*Violet, the Dark Princess*

Everyone was assembled in the Amphitheatre Hall. It was a circular building that stood seven storeys high. More than two-hundred thousand people could sit inside for a lecture.

As of now, it was full of students waiting to be told of what was to happen next. There was a platform in the center where a tall woman stood. She was a human and stood tall for her breed and gender. She waited for everyone to quiet down. The clamor of voices was deafening. But soon, it grew quiet in minutes. Everyone was quite attentive now.

Since that was established, she made an adjustment of the spectacles she wore to better her eyesight. Her earthen eyes looked around the circle to observe everyone in the crowd. She had a special knack to identify anyone she has ever seen. And she took in every face there.

Her long straight ebony hair flowed and hugged her back down past her calves where it almost touched the ground. She wore a suit skirt with a white blouse, frilled around the neck and cuffs. She wore heels. They were just for show, just as her top button was undone to reveal what little cleavage she had. Her breasts were far from being large, in size, but they were not small by any means. She did however have hips and booty to boot, and the tight navy-blue skirt did not hide what she had.

Her eyes locked with the boy who had silver eyes and golden skin. A chill ran up her spine. Her heart began to pound hard. Who was this exotic boy? She made a point to get to know him later. He was human from his look, but no human looked like that. What kingdom did he hail from?

She brought her fist to her mouth and cleared her throat. Then she clasped her hands together in front of her.

"My name is Doctor Taka, and I am a teacher here at this school. I teach the ways of healing and surgery without magic. I also work with how to use magic along with these same skill sets. For there are times when both techniques are needed," she spoke clearly and strongly for all to hear.

"I am here to explain the rules to you firsthand. You will also receive a booklet with said rules. I suggest you read them even though I explain them," she stopped to let her words sink in before continuing.

"Rule number one is the most important rule. There will be no violence 'whatsoever' done to each other. I do not believe you really want to find out the consequences of those actions," Taka paused again for effect. She noticed as she made observations that there were some looking at one another in some sort of new light, but there was also mostly contempt. She eyed the silver eyed boy. He too was observing everyone around him just as the hooded girl beside him was. Then there was Princess Catrice beside him and her guardian beside her. They were a strange group, and she was sure none were related to one another. So, why were they together? Everyone else was here with a guardian and or siblings.

Taka adjusted her spectacles again. Her demeanor grew hardened.

"Rule number two. You will show respect to everyone. Old prejudices must be put aside. You will have teachers from other races teaching classes. I realize it will take time to adapt to this new way of life we are all leading. If we can do this together, it shall be easier than working against each other. As you will find out, there are ways to settle problems. We have activities that the administration would like your help improving and naming. All this is apart of our learning process in achieving a better world for all. You are all apart of something greater now and it will be up to you to set an example to future generations of students. This year is the template of what shall be next," Taka paused and waited.

People spoke in mutters. She watched all the faces she could carefully at their reactions. One person in, particular... caught her attention. A human woman. She sneered at Taka's words. Her violet eyes were that of anger. Taka knew that girl. She was the eldest heir to The Blythe kingdom. That girl would be trouble, along with her siblings and that guardian of hers. He was a massive shadow that sat beside her in robes. There were others she noticed that would be future problems, also. She never once thought change would be easy.

"If a crime is committed here the accused will have the chance to plead their case in front of a jury of your peers. A magistrate will be appointed," she let the crowd think on those words. These were concepts unheard of before. Many years of learning lay ahead for most of them.

"There are other things to be made aware of. Today you will not be attending classes, but..." Taka raise a finger. "... you will be shown what school out of the five you shall attend, where your class is, and the seating arrangements. All by the day's end. There will be a tour in small groups throughout the day that will show you around the schools and its grounds. First when you leave here your identities will be recorded and you will sign them. When all is said and done you will be led to your dorm housing. This will be your living quarters for the entirety that you are here," she smiled as mummers went around the building.

"If there are any questions. You are welcome to come see me in my office tomorrow. I shall be there all day. Read your booklets and on your way out a map of the schools' grounds will be given to you. You are all dismissed," Taka said with a finality. She waited and watched the students. Some rushed out, most took their time. There were too many people here to go against to rush out.

Taka smiled thinly when she noticed there were a few who waited and watched also. The silver eyed boy and his companions sat there like statues as if apart of the building itself. Then there was the heir of The Blythe and her little entourage. The girl with the pigtails that sat beside her was watching the large lad from The Dhyme. The girl seemed to be head over heels crushing on him. It seemed teenage crushes were at hand. The girl was talking to her sister in a hushed tone, but the violet eyed girl was not looking to Trevor. She was watching the silver eyed boy.

So, the witch of The Blythe has an interest in him, does she. Why would she not? His exoticness is unique after all.

Then Taka watched Trevor who had noticed the pigtailed girl but was watching the silver eyed boy also. The silver eyed boy watched Taka and smiled knowingly. He was not ignoring everyone like she had thought. No! This was his way of letting the doctor know he watched also. He knew what was going on. Taka wondered about him. He was a sharp one.

"Do you students plan on staying here all day?" Taka said suddenly and startled everyone but the silver eyed boy's companions. They all rose to their feet and left.

The Tour

Welcome students to the school that will surely change your lives forever!
-*School Ambassador*

Students stood in line waiting for this weird contraption that had a lens window and a crystal that absorbed light and flashed.

After they walked by there was a piece of parchment with the seal of dragons that was to be signed. All the students signed their names to the documentation. The line up moved steadily and smoothly. There were no complications and when the students reached the end of the line, they received a small booklet with their picture and signature. All their information of who they were when they were born, height, and where they were from.

Then everyone was put into groups for their tours around the school districts. The students would be shown what doors would be closest to their classrooms and where the waypoint was located, in case of a fire.

"Glen," a voice spoke, and a hand gently rested on his shoulder.

"Yes, princess," he replied.

"I believe this is our group over here," Princess Catrice said in a low voice.

He turned away from his observations of another school group he wanted to keep in mind.

"She is Violet the Dark Princess, right?" Glen asked in a whisper. His mouth barely moved. The princess nodded.

"She has taken an interest in you, Milord," Princess Catrice whispered back. Glen frowned.

"I dislike when you call me that Princess. I think it would be wise if you were not so formal," he retorted softly. It would not do for anyone to think of him in such a standing. He was no lord, but the royal family insisted for some strange reason.

They gathered with the group and the large lad from The Dhyme walked right up to Glen and stuck out his hand in greeting.

"I am Trevor, son of Tyr Thane of The Dhyme tribes. You and I are going to be best friends," he said it as a matter-of-fact manner.

Glen could not help himself but smile at the young lord's confidence. He liked him instantly. There was a good feel about him.

"A pleasure to meet you Trevor of The Dhyme," Glen spoke sincerely. The two men clasps hands firmly.

"I sure hope we have the same class my friend," Trevor said with honesty. "This is my guardian and sister Orenda. She insisted on being my protector. We may not even be in the same class because she is a year older than I," he finished with his arm wrapped around his sister's shoulders. She rolled her eyes.

"Someone has to watch your back. The trouble you get into with women all the time," she threw back at her brother. Trevor laughed heartedly.

"See! Therefore, I love my sister so much. She has my back," Trevor praised.

"Someone has to brother or your balls would be some young lass' trophy," she laughed the last bit out. Trevor joined her.

Trevor looked to Princess Catrice' guardian. He held out his hand to her, eyes alight.

"Well, hello there my fine beauty," Trevor put on his best charming smile. Gianna just glared at him and her hand strayed to her sword.

"Alright, brother. She is definitely… not interested in you. Time to go," Orenda said hurriedly and dragged him away. Glen gave a chuckle. His companions looked at him strangely.

"Someone is in a good mood," Princess Catrice said with a smile of her own. Glen thought he saw a slight curl to Gianna's lips.

They joined with their group. A woman in a uniform just like that of Taka stood in front of everyone. Her hair was crop cut to her shoulders and she had bangs. Yellow hair like cornsilk and eyes blue like the sky. She was a short woman and all smiles.

"Hello everyone. I am Tina the School Ambassador. I will be your guide this evening. We will be the last group to wander the halls of the school. Your schedules will be in your assigned dorm rooms and you will not start schooling until the new week starts. I suggest you all brush up on the rules and your studies," she said cheerfully.

So, they walked through the school district and a brief history was explained about the school. When it was built and how.

When they arrived at their school. It was a large building of four storeys. Large windows for every class. The building was plain looking. Not like the other structures in the city.

They went in through the front entrance. A wide walkway leads right to the doors. There were four doors made of glass and metal. They went inside to a large foyer. One side had offices and hallways branched to either side and straight to the back of the school.

The ambassador took them straight ahead to the back entrance. Here was the nurse's office. Out back was a large field with posts at either end with a trail that went around in an oval shape.

The tour continued inside. They went to a gymnasium room that had mats and exercise equipment. There was a pool to swim in. They went to the only classroom that was downstairs. The ambassador named the students that would be in that class. Trevor was one of them, but his sister was not. She would be at the top level it seemed.

"Hey sis, no worries. My good friend Glen here will protect me," Trevor assured her as he leaned on Glen's shoulder.

"I will?" Glen said with raised brows.

The Ambassador listed more names. Glen and his companions were on it and more were mentioned.

"Well, you kiddies are so lucky to be in this class. See! That is a pool for the underwater monsters that will be in your class. Up above is for the flying monsters. This is a genuinely exciting class to be in. Then the students began to mutter among themselves.

They moved on upstairs to show the different classrooms. The ambassador spoke the entire time. She explained what each class was for.

Something caught Glen's attention. Someone else was following them. He went down the hallway into one of the darkened classrooms to investigate. He looked about but nothing seemed out of place. He was sure someone had come in here.

Then a hand, held his. He looked down and the hooded girl was there. He smiled. She looked up at him questioningly.

"I could have sworn someone came in here," he whispered. The girl pointed toward the door.

"You are right, Neola. We should get going," he said softly. She looked both ways in the hall then turned quickly and kissed Glen's lips. He kissed her back deeply, longingly.

Neola let out a whimper. Glen frowned.

"I know my dear. Soon," he assured her. The girl nodded and they left the room to rejoin the group.

What they did not know was that someone did go in that room and saw them together. Their body slithered down from the ceiling.

Well, that was interesting, they thought to themselves with a grin.

Dorm rooms

Sleep well and don't let the bedbugs, bite
-*School Ambassador*

It was dark when they finally got to the dorm rooms and everyone was hungry and tired.

The Ambassador showed everyone where their rooms were.

Glen went into his room and closed the door. He looked around the twenty-by-twenty room. There was a storage closet and a bathing room. The bed was large enough for three people and took up a good amount of space. There was a dresser stand against the wall where the door entrance was and a night stan on either side of the bed. The bed had a canopy with curtains. There was a single large window that opened with drapes.

The room was plain looking far from shabby. The sheets and pillows on the bed were silken. He wondered briefly, why such an expense. A desk with a chair sat in front of the window. There was a pile of papers stacked on top. Glen walked over and looked at the papers. He then shoved them in one of the drawers until the morning.

He then turned away when he heard a click to his window. He turned back and saw Neola crouched on his desk.

Glen smiled. The girl jumped into his arms and he held her for a long while. She clung to him. She breathed in his scent. She looked up at him. Glen pulled her hood away slowly. Her dark blue hair spilled out down to her waist. Indigo eyes gazed into his. Her lush pouty lips pierced together. His hand gripped her chin gently. Glen leaned in and kissed her lips. She opened her mouth to him and teased her tongue upon his. Glen groaned in pleasure and held Neola closer to him. Her small fists gripped tightly to his tunic. She panted as her arms then went around his neck and she climbed his waist with her legs.

Glen cupped his hands around her ass. Her hands then went to either side of his face and her lips ravaged his mouth.

"Love me," she whispered to him. Her voice was soft and harmonic. Glen felt soothed by her voice. Whole and complete.

He gazed longingly in those indigo orbs. He wished to be trapped in her gaze, forever!

"I love you, Neola. I always have," he breathed in her mouth.

"Love Glen, too," she said as her lips met his. He stopped and her eyes glowed.

"Now?" she asked hopefully. He opened his mouth to respond when there was a knock at the door.

"Lord Glen. May I come in?" a voice called. Glen sighed and mouthed *'I'm sorry'*.

Neola smiled pecked his lips with hers quickly. Her hood was back on and she looked back to Glen when she reached the window. She kissed her hand and blew him a kiss along with a wink of her eye. Then she disappeared.

"Come in," Glen said in a strong voice. The door opened and Princess Catrice walked in. She smiled. Her long lashes batted.

"Care to have dinner with us? Gianna is over asking Neola now," she asked sweetly. This was an indication that she would have her way regardless of one's answer. Glen nodded.

"Sounds good. I am famished," he said and patted his belly. The princess smiled.

"Good! Shall we," she said as her arm extended. He hated when the princess did this. It made other people think they were courting. He extended his arm anyway and she looped hers within. They walked out heads held high.

Dinner

Food is the fuel that feeds you!
-*Doctor Taka*

They sat in a restaurant across the street from their dorm rooms. It was a classy place, well lit and the atmosphere was pleasant. Glen, Neola, Gianna, and Princess Catrice sat at a round table draped in a red tablecloth with silver dragon patterns.

Glen felt all the eyes on him as he sat there. He knew his look was vastly different from other humans. So much so that there were a table of petite goblin girls that giggled and pointed at him. There were others that watched him.

"Mm! I would eat him up," an elven male spoke to his sister. She leaned forward and whispered as not to be overheard.

"A human, brother. Seriously!" her retort did nothing to sway the other elf.

"What does it really matter. He is a hunk of a man. So exotic. I would suck him dry," he said playfully. His sister looked at him in disgust. He only smiled and wink at Glen. Glen raised a brow and looked away. Even men were, attracted him. *How strange,* Glen thought. He wondered if men could do that sort of thing with each other.

Dinner was served with fried squid rings, white melon slices, with kelp leaves. A platter of roasted boar chopped into cubes dowsed in a dark gravy sauce with a sprinkle of shredded savory leaves. The waitress sat down a gourd of wine.

"This is elven wine from the patrons over at that table." She motioned to the elf and his sister.

Glen looked over and nodded. Then decided to walk over.

"Thank you for the wine," glen said.

"You are welcome handsome Glen," the male elf said with a bright smile. "My name is Raymond, and this lovely girl is my sister Raya," the elf introduced.

"A pleasure. Will you both kindly join us at our table.?" Glen offered.

"Don't mind if we do," Raymond said with cheer.

"But bro…" Raya tried.

"It is impolite and rude not to accept dear sister," Raymond said through gritted teeth. The elf girl sighed and agreed.

The elves joined Glen and his companions.

"My! You ladies must feel lucky to be with such a handsome man. Mm," he exaggerated his tone.

Gianna almost choked on her food.

"You kidding? This is Glen we are talking about. We have all known each other since we were children," Gianna laughed out and slapped her hand on the table.

"Oh dear. Perhaps I have been wrong. My mistake. I could have sworn you ladies were taken with him. You see I find him every attractive. As for my sister, she is not too fond of humans. The wars and all," Raymond waved his hands about. Raya sat there her brows narrowed.

"So, we are from Aeryn-Soon. Our nation thinks they are above it all and the like," the elf rolled his eyes.

"Brother! You cannot speak like that," Raya seethed. Raymond glared at his sister and she flinched. "Oh, dear sister? Who do you think will rule when father moves on? Hm! Yes, I will, and I shall bring about change to our people just as our ancestor did when she united our peoples. Of course, we fair haired and skin elves saw to it that we were dominate no less," he scrutinized.

"Very commendable Lord Raymond," Princess Catrice said and raised her glass to him.

"Ah, it is nothing. It must be my lustful appetites for sex with different races. I desire men most of all in that aspect." He smiled.

"Was it true that your nation fought against the other elves?" Glen asked.

"Yes!" Raymond said with a sigh. "So, much fighting and not enough loving. Such a waste I tell you." He leaned forward. "So, where do you all hail from? Hm!" Raymond was curious.

"From these very shores," Glen answered.

"Really!" Raymond's voice rose an octave. "This shall be an interesting school year, indeed. I for one cannot wait," he said and drank some wine.

They ate for awhile and conversation went on. Raymond was very charming and honest. Glen liked him and his sister. She may not like humans, but her brother was influencing her. She stole glances at Glen and when their eyes locked, she would give him dirty looks. Glen only smiled and nodded.

Still, other patrons eyed Glen and admired him. The monster girls more than anything eyed him up and down. He did his best to ignore the stares. His attention was spilt. He wanted to spend time elsewhere.

Suddenly, Neola stood up and made motions with her hands then bowed.

"Yes, of course. You and Glen are excused," Princess Catrice said with a bored expression. Glen stood up.

"Thank you, Princess," Glen said with a bow. The princess laughed.

"Oh, Lord Glen. You do not need permission to leave. My you are so respectful," she teased.

"Why are you leaving so soon? Handsome Glen," Raymond asked with a grin.

"To train before retiring to sleep, Lord Raymond," Glen explained.

"This girl in the cloak is your guardian I take it," Raymond mused. Glen's gaze lingered on Neola.

"Yes!" Glen said and excused himself and walked away with Neola.

The way he looked at that girl. I wonder, Raymond thought. Then he turned his attention back to the table.

First Night Together

To hold one another is wonderful!
-Glen

Glen and Neola did not go and train like they were supposed to. Instead, they went back to the dorm rooms. To Glen's room as it were.

Neola kissed Glen first thing when they reached his room. He embraced her close. She gripped tightly to his tunic never wanting to let go.

"Glen, I love," she whispered softly. Her hood fell back to reveal her perfect oval face. Her purple lips puckered. Glen's fingers trailed down her pale purple skin. So soft, so creamy. His mouth explored hers with such need that he groaned in pleasure. Her tongue responded to his every need and she did her own exploring of his mouth.

They went to lie on the bed and cuddle their lips at play. He removed his tunic and Neola's eyes glowed. She touched his chest and traced her fingers around his muscles.

She then sat up and went to remove her cloak. Glen placed his hands gently on hers and shook his head.

"Not yet. I am not ready. I am sorry Neola. Please forgive me. I know you are ready for this. I…" she placed her finger to his lips.

"Understand!" she stated "Glen, I love. Always." She smiled "Soon!" she said adamantly with a glint in her eye. Glen smiled and nodded.

"Soon!" he agreed.

She laid her head upon his broad chest and continued to trace her fingers on the muscles of his belly this time. They kissed and murmured to each other.

Neola gently placed Glen's hand upon her breast. His hand shook slightly. He was not sure what to do. All this was so new for them.

He kissed her and squeezed gently. Her gasp of pleasure enticed him. He really wanted to be with her, but felt it was not the proper time. When would that be he wondered?

"Hold me," Neola whispered passionately.

Glen wrapped his arms around her. She cuddled in so close like she was trying to be apart of him.

When they both fell fast asleep, they both had smiles.

Exploring

Exploring is a good way to observe your surroundings!
-*Violet, the Dark Princess*

Students were out and about exploring the city to familiarize themselves with their surroundings.

Glen and his companions were by chance doing that very thing.

As for Princess Catrice she wanted to go shopping. Which happened to be a surprise to the others. She never acted like the other royals in the world. But perhaps, she was putting on a façade for the other princesses. Either way, they were all going shopping.

Here they were in a fashion shop with dresses and suits. Thus far they were the only customers in the shop.

"Us, ladies shall be trying on dresses for tonight's event. There is a ball to welcome the students at our schools," Princess Catrice revealed. They all knew this ahead of time. The princess did have a hand in organizing the curriculum. They had their own missions. To mingle and get to know the students and their prospects. Observe and catalogue their behavior and power levels, if any.

They are here to play dress up, now.

"You shall have a dress too, Neola," the princess said. The young girl shook her hooded head. The princess gave a sideways glance. Neola knew that look and nodded.

"Good girl. You shall look stunning when I am done with you," the princess grinned. She then chose a few dresses and went into a room with the other girls.

Glen waited outside for them to finish. He listened to them talk and tilted his head.

Did he just hear Gianna giggle? The princess sure did when it was girl time. She rarely smiled or laughed in public unless it emphasised the conversation, she was engaged in.

"Oh, come on Neola. It will look ravishing on you. There are men here to be had. Explore them. You do not need to be their mates. Just have fun with them," the princess chided. The princess laughed. "Do not shake your head. You never know what the future holds, my dear. Now, try the dress on."

More talk of the ball and who they may meet and greet came up. Compliments and teasing pasted between the girls.

"Excuse me, Lord Glen," a male voice interrupted. Glen looked over at the proprietor.

"Sven. Good day to you good sir," Glen said, and they shook hands.

"Your suit and your other item are ready," the tailor said. "This way," he motioned with his hand.

Glen followed him into another room. He was led to another room after that. It was the man's workshop. There were rows upon rows of shelving with a multitude of fabrics. Sven showed Glen his suit.

"It will fit you perfectly, Milord," Sven assured him. "So, will this," the tailor held up the other item. Glen nodded his approval.

"Very good then," Sven said. "Glad you approve good Lord." He then grabbed a hanging rod. It was made of metal that was wrapped in a cotton rope. It had a looped hook so it could hang from a bar or peg. The rest of its body or two bodies, twisted in the same triangular shape. The one item was hung on one and the suit on the other. Then they were wrapped in a fabric bag. Glen thanked him and went back to wait for the girls. He had already paid for his items ahead of time and spared no expense.

He made it back in time as the girls came out of the room all smiles and cheer, but for Neola. Could not tell under that hood of hers.

"Well, Glen. What do you have there?" the princess motioned toward what he held.

"My suit," Glen replied.

"Oh, is that so? May we see it?" she asked with a hard stare.

Glen smiled bitterly.

"You may, when at the Ball," he said. He turned and walked away. "If you ladies do not mind. I have to get ready," he threw over is shoulder.

"I never thought that man would keep a secret from us," Princess Catrice mused.

Neola looked to the princess. The princess nodded to her and Neola left to follow Glen.

"Princess. What of the suit you got for him?" Gianna asked concerned.

The princess sighed.

"I guess it will have to wait for some other kind of event," she said in disappointment.

"Princess. Are you sure you want to do this?" Gianna questioned.

The princess looked to her guardian, her friend.

"Yes! No worries dear. It will not interfere with our relationship," she said with a sly smile.

A Brief Embrace

A hug can be one of the greatest signs of affection!
-Princess Catrice

Glen waited in his room. He paced to and fro with his hands behind his back. His thoughts were on tonight. He really did not want to go but was obligated. He would do this for his princess, Gianna his friend and Neola. The girl he was fond of.

A sound by his window. He looked up and there Neola was crouched on his desk. She leaped from the desk into his arms. Their lips met. He crushed her to him. She in turn clung to him as she liked to do with her fists curled in his tunic.

"Glen, I love," she breathed into his mouth. They kissed more.

"Neola," he groaned her name in passion. Neola began to whimper. She fell to the ground.

"Glen, I need," she gasped. Glen knelt and held her.

"Neola. What is wrong?" he asked worriedly. She bit her lip and grabbed his hand. She looked him with wary eyes. Then she brought his hand within her cloak between her thighs.

"I ache," she choked out. Glen felt her warmth and wetness and blushed. He hugged her close.

"Soon, my love. I promise," Glen assured.

She breathed him in to steady her shaking. His scent was like a drug to her. She breathed him in again.

Glen stood up and brought her with him.

"I have something for you," he said and went into the storage closet. He brought out the bagged package from earlier that day.

Neola eyes went wide. She rushed over and Glen handed her the gift to her.

"Mine. Dress," she said. Glen nodded.

"Now we must prepare for tonight and what comes after," he insinuated. Her mouth dropped. She took a deep breath and smiled. She gave Glen a quick kiss on the lips. He grabbed her hand and pointed to the door.

"You must use the door. Not the window. Just so your dress does not get ruined," he said gently as he touched her chin. She nodded, then rushed out to her own room.

Violet

I will have the best dress there!
-*Violet, the Dark Princess*

Violet, the Dark Princess of The Blythe was being dressed by her servants. She had bought a mansion near her school.

She detested the dorm rooms with all those other races. She did not tolerate the weaker peoples. They were worthless in her mind. She hated the elves. The pointed eared freaks. Her people would take their ears and sell them to the highest bidder. The women were enslaved and done with however their owners wanted. She cared less about the other races and this school was not going to change her mind about any of it.

All Violet cared about at this moment was how she would look for the Ball. This was a time to socialize before school would start with classes. She wondered briefly as to what form of education would be taught.

When she had finished with her hair and dress. She admired herself in a full-bodied mirror.

Violet's dress was the colour of her name's sake. It was patterned in spirals in rich jewels of sapphire. Her dress hugged her form down and bloomed out at her ankles in a frill. There were no sleeves. It just wrapped around her chest where her large breasts seemed like they wanted to over spill at any moment. She liked that her bosom revealed so much. Most eyes would be on her anyway.

Her cheeks were blushed, and lips were darkened black to emphasis her title. Kohl was rubbed around her eyes to darken them and above her eye lids were shaded violet. Her lashes were darkened and full of length.

Her violet hair was weaved with gold ornate wire down to spiral around her one shoulder.

She smiled brightly, her teeth white and clean. Her violet eyes gave off a hazy glow. She was ready.

"What is your plan tonight sis?" Poppy asked. She was dressed in a pink frilly dress that seemed more for a child then a girl her age.

"I plan on nabbing me a man," Violet replied still staring into the mirror.

Poppy put bright red rouge on her lips. Her cheeks were blushed like her sister's and her hair was in pigtails but also in buns. She was cute as a doll.

Poppy frowned at herself.

"Why was I not blessed with boobs like you and Rose," Poppy complained and pouted.

"Oh, dear. You will grow some soon. Be patient Poppy. You are still young yet," Violet answered.

"Sis. I love you. You are good to me," Poppy said.

"I love you too, Poppy. You are my sister and I trust you most of all. There is no doubting your loyalty," Violet praised and hugged her sister. She then kissed her cheek.

"Ewe! Sis!" Poppy screeched and wiped her cheek. The two girls giggled.

"So, Poppy. Do you have your eyes set on a special someone?" Violet asked.

Poppy turned red.

"Maybe," she replied.

"Perhaps it is Trevor," Violet teased.

Poppy went red further.

"He is a good choice for you. You better nab him in a hurry. I hear he likes to have a lot of women in his bed," Violet said.

"I am not ready for that yet," Poppy retorted.

"Well, he is handsome in a rugged way. He is royalty and you like him. Just get his attention," Violet said.

"I will try," Poppy said nervously.

"Well. Let us go and have a good time sis," Violet said and took Poppy by the hand.

Trevor

The wolf wants to prowl!
-Trevor

Trevor had just finished dressing himself for the Ball. He was looking forward to meeting the many women there. He hoped to bring one back to his room for the night.

He grinned at himself in the mirror. Damn, he was a hunk. He never had a problem getting a girl in his bed. He wanted to chase girls, but they mostly chased him. He liked that too. He was all about sex. He hungered for it. What was he to do if he ever married? Would he have to stop seeing other women? He did not like that idea at all. He had to be careful with his addiction to sex. He always wore his cock sheath. It prevented pregnancy and disease and still allowed extreme pleasure for both partners. He carried it everywhere he went as a precaution.

He fixed his bowtie a final time and gave a wolfish grin in the mirror. He could not wait to show all the monster ladies what a human could do in the bedroom.

He paused a moment to gather his thoughts. He had to control himself, his anger. He took a deep breath. The other human nations he did his best not to loathe. A thousand years ago The Blythe had come to his people. They wanted an alliance to fight the monsters of the world. At the time it was his tribe that encountered them. They were in talks at first. But later, his tribe turned against them. The Dhyme have always had spies in the other nations and knew their languages. It was discovered that The Blythe was culling all creatures and had even betrayed other nations and took them for their own. Those small nations no longer existed and shall never be mentioned in history.

As the story goes his tribe killed all the soldiers and made it look like monsters had done it. After a while, a new patrol of soldiers came looking for their brethren. Trevor's people told them that they had not seen them. That the lands were poisoned by shadow creatures that rotted the land. On the border between the lands, it seemed that way with the black mushrooms that guarded their borders and the dark fey. For the most part the story was believed as when The Blythe kept sending soldiers to the borders. Always the bodies were mutilated. Even allowed a single survivor once. He was a raving lunatic after the traumatic events. The effects of poison were not a lie but the People of The Dhyme helped in slaughtering the scouts and spies.

Trevor had no regrets about his people's actions. They did what was necessary to protect themselves. Besides, Trevor would do what it took to keep his people's alliance with the Sihronn, people of the Glaciers. He had met with them once. They had an odd scent and could not be seen under all the furs they wore. Goods were traded between the two peoples and few of Trevor's people knew what they truly looked like and were tight lipped about it. Maybe one would be at the Ball. He would know by their scent.

Maybe he would bring two girls home or three. He was especially horny. He needed to sate his hunger so he could concentrate in class. It was not time for classes yet anyhow. Time to party.

Trevor gave himself a last wolfish grin and then left his dorm room for the Ball.

Rose

I will out do my sister!
-*Rose*

Like every other student, Rose readied herself for tonight's events. Not only did she want to outshine her sister, but the other women as well. She cared less for this trivial school system and making peace. She only cared about the parties and the sex afterward.

"Miles. How do I look?" Rose asked her guardian.

"Ravishing, my Queen," he said sincerely.

It turned her on when he called her that. She did plan on being queen one day. She just had to rid her sister who was the rightful heir. Then she could work on her slutty harem mother who sat on the throne.

It irked her that her mother had so many men at her disposal. Each of her siblings had a different father, it was gross. The old Regent Toraegon had been her husband until he died in battle and in her mother's grief, she built a harem to have orgies with as many men as possible.

Violet is the Regent's daughter, so that made her not only the oldest but rightful heir to the throne. If something were to happen to Violet, then she is the next in line who could take the throne. Her own father was a duke after all. He owned the largest lands and had a larger force than the other dukes.

There was another problem. Her sister Poppy. She had a really, close relationship with Violet. This bothered Rose for some reason. No one knew who Poppy's father was. Even if he still lived or if he was just one of the many men from one of the orgies. Poppy was a special girl. She did not look like any of the other people of The Blythe. She looked mixed breed to Rose. It was a possibility. Their mother was a whore after all. The woman enjoyed nothing more than to have her legs spread by any man.

What disturbed Rose the most was the outrageous rumours of her mother having sex with monster men. She let out a small chuckle at the thought. Ridiculous! Her mother would never do such a thing. That woman loathed everyone even humans. Although… she shook her head. No more of these thoughts would she have. Not tonight.

She admired her crimson gown with a side slip. Her large breasts showed all their glory to the point where one could almost see her nipples. She enjoyed the stares that went her way and it turned her on when man desired her, and she knew they could never have her. Her dark auburn hair draped loose down her back. She had pink eyeshadow and rose petal lips. Full and kissable. Her ass was round full and bouncy stiff. She touched the tattoo on her breast. It was of her house. The house that would rule a nation one day.

Rose backed up into Miles and rubbed her ass into his crotch.

"Am I desirable my love?" she demanded. Her guardian gulped.

"Yes, my Queen," he panted out and she felt his response through his trousers.

"Mm! Miles you are growing so hard for me. If I were to relieve you now. Would you be able to fuck me later tonight after the party?" she questioned passionately. She knew damn well he could, but she liked to hear it regardless.

"Yes, my Queen, love of my life," he groaned. Just what she wanted to hear.

Rose turned around and went to her knees and undid his trousers. He looked on in surprise.

"Would you like this or do you want to drip down my legs all night at the party?" she asked. Not that she would let him decide anyway. She wanted a taste, and she would have it.

"What ever best suits, my queen," he replied.

Good answer, she thought and put him in her mouth.

Miles let out a deep groan as she sucked gently on him. She knew how to work him up and he would explode in no time and then she would make him do it again. That way he could fuck her a good long time later.

Just as she knew it would happen. He exploded in her mouth and she swallowed every bit of his succulent seed. She loved the taste of him.

She stood up. She was going to make him shoot in her mouth again but changed her mind. She wanted him to drip down her legs tonight. She wanted the monsters to smell his scent upon her. To let them know she was claimed.

She turned around and lifted her dress.

"Now, fuck me please," she begged him. His still hard cock entered her, and she gasped in wondrous pleasure.

"Oh, Miles fuck me my love," she demanded. Miles drove into her hard and fast.

"Oh, my queen," Miles groaned out through gritted teeth. This triggered her into ecstasy.

"Oh, Miles. Do it with me. Give me that baby," she cried out.

Then he exploded within her. She reveled in their pleasure. She could make him go again. She wanted to. She would wait. Tonight, he would give her such pleasures like none other ever could. He was the man to have pleased her. The other men she had been with hurt her and it was over quickly. She never once felt any pleasure. One man was so quick that it confused her. She was sure he entered her, but he was a two-pump chump and collapsed in exhausting. What kind of man did that?

Then she met Miles and she had an instant connection to him. The first time they made love he brought her to such heights she never dreamed of. She knew then that he would be her Regent and they would make the most beautiful babies.

Miles regrettably pulled out of her. Rose reached up with one arm around his neck and she tilted her head and their lips met. He kissed her deeply. She loved the taste of his mouth. Her heart fluttered from how he looked at her. She loved him with all her heart. The way he made her feel was a miracle.

Now, she just wanted to stay here in her dorm room with him, never to leave. She sighed.

"My love, we must we go?" she wanted to hear him say *no* and knew he would not. He took her duties seriously and she understood that duty had to come at some point.

"Sorry, my love, my Queen. Duty calls," he breathed in her mouth. He kissed her lightly and then held her close. She let herself be vulnerable in his arms. She felt safe from the harsh world. For the time being at lest.

Finding A View

Finding the best observation point is key!
-Aeryn-Soon saying

Raymond and his sister Raya arrived at the Royal Ball Hall extremely early. They happened to be the first guests to arrive. Of course, they were hours earlier than needed.

"Why are we here so damn early, brother," Raya said in annoyance. Her petite face all scrunched up.

That is because, dear sister, I wish a spectacular view of the Hall to watch every guest that comes in. It is a tactical position," he explained.

Raya huffed. She was dressed in a simple forest green dress. Her golden hair was tied in a single ponytail with a silver clasp. She did not wear makeup and cared little about how she looked for everyone else. She had no interest in boys or making girl friends. She just wished she were at home.

They walked up a set of stairs that led way up three storeys and Raymond went to the top level. The heeled shoes Raya wore hurt her feet and she could not wait to sit down to take them off. What idiot would come up with such an idea anyway. You must need some form of training to be able to walk properly in these things.

They sat at a table that was across from the entrance, which gave them a clear view. They would see every single person that walked through into the Hall.

The ballroom was a large circular room rich in ornate fashion. Brightly lit with not a single shadow to be seen. A job well done! Raymond was impressed.

Raya slouched in her chair. She had no interest in being here whatsoever and showed it.

"Dear sister, please try not to be such a bump on a log. Mm!" Raymond said.

"Stupid dragons making us be somewhere we do not want to be," Raya muttered. Raymond chuckled.

"Not I dear sister. I rather enjoy being here. Think of it this way. We get to experience something no one else gets to. We get to live in a different world with so many other things to explore. The people. Where else in this world could we meet so many different people in one spot. I find this glorious," he said the last sentence musically.

"Whatever!" Raya said miserably and folded her arms. She thought about his words as she always did, and he was right. This was an exciting opportunity. Maybe she should get to know others. It was working for her brother. Last night at dinner was nice and Glen and his companions were nice people. Glen was handsome… she shook her head. No humans. No way. She waited for the ball to start.

Aeryn-Soon

Only united can we defeat our enemies!
-Aeryn-Soon, Queen of the Elves

She had successfully united all the elven nations together as one. They had made her Queen of the Elves. A title she would more than prove worthy of many times over.

Aeryn-Soon had defeated the human invasions repeatedly. Soon the humans turned on each other and their forces became fractured and overcome by the elves.

The humans were driven back to where they came from and had not come back. Peace was established with other monster nations and fae, *along with the faeries. It was a grand time for the elves. To be without war at last was a blessing.*

There were hundreds of years of peace for the elves. They traded with other nations and even other culture practices came. Monsters were even allowed to live amongst the elves. There was equality and friendship bonds. Even inter-marriages. The offspring were loved and cherished.

But darkness loomed overhead once again. There was word that humans were organizing attacks along the borders of the kingdom.

The Queen wanted to parley with the humans. To try and prevent a war. To reason with them.

A location was made along the border for a meeting. The queen was escorted along with her most trusted general, Riven. He was a hero to the people.

When they got to their location Riven begged his queen not to go into the cave. He felt that it was a trap. A lure to destroy all that she had built. But she would not hear of it. She believed in trying to work out a peace treaty with them. It was worth the risk. The humans deserved a chance to prove themselves.

So, it was decided. They would move on into what may be a trap. When they reached the meeting point it turned out to be a trap. But not by humans, elves. They were betrayed. The queen was slain and fell into a crevice and all her soldiers killed. Only General Riven escaped. He had killed the last of the traitors.

When he reached the capital, he informed the council what had happened, and the dark elves were blamed and so were other monster kind. War broke out once again.

The dark elves were driven out and slaughtered without mercy. Mixed breeds were culled. It soon became a crime to mix with the other races. The Aeryn-Soon elves became the largest and most powerful nation. None were trusted and again they were at war with humans. The fair elves were on the verge of destruction until the dragons came. Then everything changed. Riven excepted the dragons demands. Only to save his people.

Taka

This school is our greatest hope!
-*Doctor Taka*

Taka had stayed at her office all day answering questions and readying paperwork. Only close to a hundred students came to see her. A few boys just wanted to lust over her, and she reminded them to read their rule booklets.

'Teacher and student were forbidden from having any kind of relationship whatsoever except that of teacher and student during class times.'

Poor lads. When they left, they were like broken hearted puppies! It was adorable. But as both a teacher and a doctor, she had no time for such things.

Now however, she was at home getting ready to go to the Ball herself. She dressed in a white gown. It was a little cliché, but she was a doctor after all. She wore white gloves to her elbows to match. She darkened her lips to a blue. She wore black boots. She wanted comfort not the discomfort of 'killer heels' as she liked to call them.

Taka took a final look at herself and decided it was time to go. She left her office and walked down the street.

"Hey taka. Wait up," a voice cried out to her. Taka turned around to see Tina running toward her. The Ambassador's shoulder cropped blonde hair bounced about. The doctor waited for her friend to catch up. Tina stopped beside her and took a few moments to catch her breath.

"Thank you for waiting Taka," the ambassador said gratefully, her blue eyes sparkled.

They soon continued to walk.

"My Tina, you look pretty tonight," Taka said politely.

"Why tank you, Taka. I must go to all the Halls tonight to observe how the students interact with each other," Tina explained.

"Oh my, Tina you have a busy night. Would you like for me to accompany you?" Taka asked.

"Would you?" Tina asked excitedly.

"Of course, I will," Taka said.

"That would be so great. Thank you again Taka," the Ambassador said cheerfully.

They walked on talking about what they thought might happen at the party. They hoped for some sort of excitement.

They arrived at their destination and went inside. They would do meet and greets when everyone started to show up.

Looked like everyone was doing last minute arrangements. In another hour or so people would show up and the party would begin.

Taka noticed that two elves were already here. Interesting. Why, it was the perfect spot to observe everything around. How clever of them. Taka smiled.

She turned to Tina and pointed to the to the sparkling spirit's fountain.

"Shall we?"

Tina grinned.

"Oh, most definitely," she laughed.

They went and filled up their glasses and drank the booze. Sparkling spirits was a faerie brew that if one drank too much, which mind you was about three glasses, would knock you cold. Seemed these two ladies intended to do just that.

Glen

Bathing is cleansing and relaxing!
-Glen

Glen removed his clothing and threw them in a wicker basket. He would find time later to wash those.

Glen went into the bathing room. He stepped down and slowly lowered himself into the steamy hot waters. It stung his skin at first. Soon, it began to sooth the aches in his muscles. He was tense.

His thoughts drifted in a hazy fashion. He needed to relax.

He thought about Neola. She was ready to have sex with him. This he knew. Not just because she said it with her own words, it was how her body responded to him. The wetness of her thighs. How she wanted to explore him. Glen sighed softly.

He wanted her so bad that it hurt. His chest clenched in pain. He grew hard thinking about her. He was very much in love with her.

They had started their romance over a year ago. But keep it secret. Especially from the princess. Everyone knew how she felt about him. What her felt from Princess Catrice was not love, but lust. The princess desired him because he was told by her father that he was of royal blood. When he was found out in the wilds a sigil was in his procession that made it so. To this day he wondered where he had come from.

Neola, how I love you so, Glen thought. He promised about tonight and he would keep that promise whether he was ready or not. But still, what was he to do. He had no idea how to please a woman. Or anything about sex. He has never seen a woman's body. What was he to do? All these thoughts preyed on him.

Glen sunk down under the water. He let the heat wash over him and soon it began to sooth him. It took some time. Glen did relax for awhile.

Later, he dressed in his suit of navy blue trimmed in silver. With the sigil crest on his left breast. He even tied his hair back. He looked at himself in the mirror. His suit was clean and in prime condition. He was ready.

There was a knock on his door.

"Glen. Are you ready to go?" It was the princess. Glen opened his door.

"Oh, good! You are ready. Time to leave," she said and turned away.

Neola stepped out of her room in her cloak. Glen smiled. Gianna looked perplexed.

"She is not going like that is she?" Gianna asked.

"Of course not, silly," Catrice scolded. We have a plan remember. Gianna rolled her eyes.

"When do you ever inform me of your plans, princess 'spur of the moment'." Gianna retorted with a glare.

"Oh, never mind that," the princess said annoyed with a wave of her hand.

Gianna looked to Glen.

"You believe this?" she said to him.

Glen just shook his head and smiled. He followed the three women to the carriage that awaited them.

It was a short ride to the Hall. They all got out but Neola. The princess turned to her.

"Now, wait a little while. Do your thing and then come in. You will surprise everyone my dear," Princess Catrice said excitedly. Glen winked to Neola and Gianna nodded. They were off to the Ball.

At the Ball

A time to dance;
And a time to fraternize!
-Ambassador Tina

What a night it shall be as the guests poured in to be seen and to observe everyone else. Tonight, would be the only party for an awfully long time. In three days, time school would begin. Two days to read your rule book and schedules. To rest of course. This would be the only free time for a while also.

So, the students had this moment to live it up and party their faces off. They were even allowed to drink the spirits.

Trevor walked in and saw Glen and his companions and went to greet them.

"Hey buddy. Are you ready to party it up? I sure am. Maybe, get a few notches under that belt of yours?" Trevor said with enthusiasm as he wrapped his arm around Glen's shoulder. Glen raised his brows.

"Oh, come on man. There are so… many honeys around to taste. Live a little," Trevor suggested.

"You are a lustful fellow, Trevor. Is there anything else you think about besides women?" Glen asked with interest. Trevor pulled away and put a finger to his dimpled chin in thought.

"I do not believe so. Ah! What does it matter? Women are life my friend," Trevor boasted. Trevor gave a playful punch to Glen's shoulder.

"Glen. It is time," Princess Catrice said motioning toward the entrance. Glen nodded and looked.

"Time for what?" Trevor asked.

Glen made a shush sound out of the corner of his mouth. Trevor observed the entrance. His eyes bulged out and his mouth went slack at what he saw.

"By the Wolf," Trevor breathed. "Who the hell is that beauty?"

Glen smiled knowingly and walked toward the woman who had just entered. Their eyes met and they gazed longingly at one another.

She was dressed in a purple gown trimmed in silver with a crest on her left breast. It was a creature that looked to have many forms, always changing. Her long raven like hair draped almost to the ground. Her firm small breasts were perky and showed a glimpse of cleavage. Two slips revealed her golden skinned legs. Her silver eyes caught the attention of everyone around. She looked every bit like Glen, only she was a woman.

Glen bowed to her. She nodded.

"Milady. May I have this dance?" Glen asked. She nodded.

"Easy Glen. Let me show you how it's done bro…" Trevor interrupted. The woman ignored him and took Glen's hand. Glen chuckled.

"You sure showed me, Trevor," Glen chuckled.

Trevor grabbed his chest pretending an arrow struck his heart.

"Oh, my heart has been struck," he groaned and fell to the ground. That brought chuckles and giggles from the crowd.

Glen walked to the dance floor with his date.

"You look so beautiful Neola that words escape me," He complimented. People in the crowd heard and word soon got around as to who she was. Glen leaned in and whispered.

"As beautiful as you are now. I still prefer your original form, my love." His breath was hot upon her neck. She blushed.

They danced and all attention was upon them as was intended.

They glanced around at peoples faces to note their reactions. Princess Catrice was impressed but there was a look that bothered Glen. The way she observed them. She was not looking at them but something on them. He wondered if it was the crests they wore. Did she know something about them? He had to find out at some point in time. The princess was clearly annoyed about something.

Glen pushed it from his mind, for now. He would address it at the earliest opportunity.

He would enjoy this moment with Neola. She smiled the entire time, but he knew she struggled with her emotions. He saw the ever so slight muscle movements in her jaw. The tweaks in her nose. The small twitches in her eyelids. She would make tapping motions on Glen's hand with her fingers to communicate with him. It was something that they came up with. Only they knew of it. It was their secret.

Music filled the hall and Glen, and Neola were the center of attention as they danced. A dance never seen before. This is how they dance here in Tulladiss. It was elegant yet wild.

Princess Catrice watched them careful. Her attention was fully on them. Gianna looked around at everyone else. She was always on edge ready for action. As, much as Gianna praised these efforts for peace among the nations, there were always plots in the making. Trust was earned and even then, there was betrayal. This she had learned the hard way during her training.

"Did Neola just laugh," Gianna said keeping her voice low. The princess nodded in suspicion. Gianna knew this mood. Her princess hid it well from the others in the room. She was her guardian and knew how to read her princess well enough when she was annoyed inside.

Gianna looked to Glen and Neola. They seemed to be having fun. Were they acting for the crowd or... did that bother the princess? Gianna sighed slightly. The princess always wanted what she could never have. She was told by the council that she could not marry him, because of his lineage. That there was a roll for him to play. The princess was not to interfere with any relationship that he may develop. Gianna knew the princess planned on defying those orders. She was obsessed with wanting his child. Could not blame her Gianna supposed. Glen was a very handsome man. She even had dirty thoughts about him, and it did not help when the princess talked about him and the things, she planned to do with him.

The dance was over. Glen and Neola came to join them.

"How did we do out there," Glen asked.

"Fine," Princess Catrice said abrupt. She took a deep breath. "The two of you have their attention. They will be watching the two of you closely now and there is a particular person who may even be terribly angry right about now," Catrice smiled mischievously. "You both did well. Neola. This is how you shall be at school every day," the princess ordered. Neola nodded.

"Speak child," the princess mocked. Neola's eyes went wide, and her mouth dropped open in shock.

"Well?" the princess asked with raised brows.

Neola narrowed her brows. She sneered and stomped her foot, made a rude hand motion. She then grabbed Glen's hand and they walked away. Glen frowned at the princess as he left. Why had the princess been so rude he wondered?

"That was uncalled for, princess!" Gianna stated.

"I know that," Catrice snapped. There it was. Her jealousy. The princess took a deep shuddering breath.

"I apologies, Gianna. I was out of line."

"Shall we go mingle, princess? Get to know the other students and teachers?" Gianna suggested.

"I suppose so," the princess replied. "I will get what I want. I assure you; Gianna and you will join me. This I have decided."

"Excuse me, princess?" Gianna wondered.

The princess giggled.

"Oh, I am terribly sorry, Gianna. Did I not tell you? When I finally have sex with Glen you will be there with us. You will fuck him also," Catrice elaborated.

Gianna was in shock for two reasons. First, her princess wanted her to be in a threesome. Second, the princess swore. She never said such words. This said something about how far she was willing to go with Glen. Gianna suddenly had a dreaded feeling about all this.

"But Princess it is forbidden to," Gianna tried.

"Why? The council say so. My father says so. Glen is only human after all," the princess stressed.

True! He was human, but what if he was something more? Like magic was bestowed upon him by the dragons. Would that make him dangerous?

Gianna put it out her mind and joined the princess in the crowd.

Fury

Anger clouds the mind;
Fury fuels action!
-*Violet, the Dark Princess*

Violet stood on the second level terrace and watched everyone as they milled about. She identified who would be a threat to her the most. It was a game she liked to play.

Poppy stood beside her. An ever-faithful loyal sister. Violet loved the girl very much. Poppy was the only person she could rely on besides her bodyguard who was always close by hidden in the shadows somewhere. He would report to her when necessary. He was also her spy. She would see him later tonight and from there plan on her next strategy.

When she had first came in, she had noticed two dirty elves on the top level. Violet knew they were scoping out everyone who walked in. It was a smart strategy. She wished she had thought of it. Raymond and Raya were their names. The Dark Princess marked them as a threat.

As she observed the audience her eyes strayed to Glen continuously. He intrigued her. Besides, he could help her create a strong heir to her throne. After that she did not care who he fucked, if she got what she wanted. She even entertained the idea of marriage. To lay claim to such an exotic man as him would make her extremely popular among her people. Maybe even among other kingdoms. This sudden thought brewed ideas she would explore later.

"Look, Poppy. Your little crush is conversing with Glen. Wonder what they are talking about?" Violet asked.

Poppy shrugged her shoulders. Her eyes were glued to Trevor like a lovesick puppy.

How endearing, Violet thought with a smile. She wondered briefly how she could help her sister to attain the man she desired. Violet would see what could be done to help.

There was a change in atmosphere of the crowd suddenly. Violet gazed down toward the entrance. Her eyes widened. She was stunned at what she saw. Not much surprised Violet but this was totally unexpected. The woman she observed was just like Glen. Violet watched as Glen greeted her. Then she knew. It was that cloaked guardian of his.

"There are fucking two of them," Violet seethed in outrage. She crushed her glass of spirits. Poppy gripped her arm.

"Sis. Please calm down," the girl tried to console her sister.

As violet watched Glen and Neola, her rage grew. The gall. Her plans snatched away just like that. Before she could even plan anything.

"What the Fuck!" Violet almost screamed. The people around her were watching now and whispering. She ignored them as her eyes glowed.

"Violet, not here," Poppy tried again.

"I am going to put a stop to this farse," Violet gritted. She tried to climb the rail when a dark shadowy cloaked figure appeared absorbed Violet and was gone.

Poppy breathed a sigh of relief.

"Hey everyone," she said with a weak wave. "Sisters huh."

The crowd moved away from Poppy. The girl frowned and turned to lean on the rail.

"Oh! I will never make friends if this keeps happening," Poppy groan in misery.

Eavesdropping

All you need to do is listen carefully!
-Trevor

After Glen and Neola went to dance Trevor stayed nearby princess Catrice. He was curious about the princess and what she might be up to. She was a political power after all.

He watched his best friend dance with the most extraordinary woman that has ever walked this world. Trevor thought he understood why the two of them seemed inseparable. Good for them! It made Trevor smile. Glen already had a girl before he even came to this school.

Trevor's true focus however was on princess Catrice. He listened and waited for her to speak.

Things got interesting when Glen and his girl returned to the princess. The princess said something that sounded demeaning. Trevor guessed that Neola could not speak. Strange. He never perceived the princess to be unkind in such a way. Then it went in another direction. Then he understood. The princess wanted Glen for herself and she seemed to be a little kinky and wanted her guardian to join in.

Trevor took a sip of his drink and moved on to mingle with other people. He searched around just as others did. Some people were keeping to themselves. Trevor was surprised there was interaction. He was glad some of the other races were intermingling. He wanted in on the action.

He went outside on a terrace and there was a group of ladies prime for the picking.

He sauntered over.

"Hello ladies," Trevor said with as much charm possible.

The girls blushed and giggled. He bowed and introduced himself.

"My name is…"

"We know who you are, Trevor," One of the girls said. She was an orc of pale green, grey skin and well muscled. He could tell she was a warrior. He was interested most definitely. He looked into her earth brown eyes. Her black hair was shaved on both sides while tied back. She had a nice form with breasts that were more then a hand full. Her dress was a black gown that showed her abs and gave a peek at her pelvis. She was desirable in Trevor's eyes.

She stood close to him. She was almost his height and Trevor, not a small man by any means. He was a giant among his own kind.

"You are handsome, for a human," the orc woman ran a finger down his muscled chest. She gripped his arms and squeezed hard. Trevor smiled and flexed. The orc grinned impressed.

"You have muscles like iron," she breathed. "I like very much."

"You are a very beautiful woman," Trevor breathed back and leaned in to kiss her. She let him kiss her and her mouth opened to him. She understood what he said. He called her woman. Not orc or pig. Woman. He said she was beautiful and meant it. She knew it was about sex and accepted it. Besides if he could satisfy her. She would sleep with him again. They finished their kiss and the other girls asked how it was. The orc smiled.

"Try him and find out if you like," the orc woman said with a grin. She was sexy with her toothy grin and those two small tusks that suck out from her bottom lip.

"Don't mind if I do," one of the other girls said. She was a feline of some sort. She wore a silky looking red gown that did little to hide anything she had. It covered a small part of her large breasts then cross strapped down to two pieces of cloth that covered next to nothing of her privates. Those yellow eyes caught him. She had tuffs of fur on the backs on her arms and legs. Her tail was jet black and smooth to the touch as it swished up and touched his arm. She purred in his face. Her tongue came out and licked his lips. Trevor opened his mouth to her, and she quickly ravaged it. Her kiss was great also.

How he wanted these women. They pulled away after a short time. She had a feline smile.

"You are a great kisser too," he complemented her.

"My turn," a third girl giggled. She was smaller than the other girls and beautiful also. He knew she was a goblin by her dark green skin. She leaped upon him her lips meet his. She opened her mouth to him, and Trevor went in with his tongue. She was dressed in hides that he could easily just move aside to feel her private parts.

The goblin girl leaned back and looked at the other girls.

"I am going home with him tonight. He made me wet," she confessed with a grin. "He feels large below the belt too," the goblin girl revealed.

The orc and feline looked to each other in surprise.

"Well, Trevor. Will you take us home for the night," the orc woman asked.

"I most definitely will," Trevor hollered as he spun the goblin girl around in his arms.

"Shall we ladies?" Trevor said with a charming wolfish grin.

He carried the goblin girl on his back and had the other two women on each arm as he left the party. He ignored the gawking stares.

"Who cares what they think!" Trevor stated with a smile. "I am in the company of three beautiful women, and I am the luckiest guy here."

Violet's Shadow

Fuck this self-righteous shit!
-Violet, the Dark Princess

She suddenly appeared in an alley some distance away from the Ball. Violet was furious with her captor.

Her eyes glowed with power and energy wrapped itself around her fists as she clenched at her sides. She attacked swinging. Her energy phased through her shadowy opponent and smashed into the wall of the building. Two holes were empaled in the wall. Shale like pieces of brick littered the ground.

"Are we calm now, mistress," the figure asked.

"Why did you take me away, Garm?" Violet screamed.

"If not, someone would have been hurt or even killed and you are accountable for your actions, princess. I am your guardian. I must protect you," his hollowed voice boomed. A hint of his annoyance.

"We have to go back. You left my sister behind you oaf," Violet said and smacked his arm. He sighed.

"Only if you stay calm," he retorted.

"I will behave Garm. I promise," Violet assured him. He nodded. Violet reached out.

"Come on. Give momma a hug," she teased playfully, her whole demeaner changed.

She was embraced by the shadowy form and was suddenly back beside her sister and Garm was gone in a blink of an eye before anyone could realize what had happened.

Violet leaned on the rail beside her sister.

"I am sorry, Poppy. It will not happen again," Violet said.

"It is alright sis. No harm done," Poppy replied.

"So, did I miss anything interesting?" Violet asked carefully.

"Just Trevor leaving with three girls that I am sure he is going to fuck," Poppy said sadly. Violet sighed.

"I am so sorry to hear that Poppy. I know how much you like him," the Dark Princess did her best to console her sister. Poppy gave her a hug.

"No big deal. If I, have you with me. I am good sis," Poppy sniffled into her sister's shoulder. Violet felt the wetness and knew Poppy was more upset than she let on.

"I love you too, Poppy, my dear," Violet said with a smirk. She would try to help her sister get the man of her dreams.

Evening Stroll

> Nothing like a nightly walk to clear the cobwebs out of your head!
> *-Ambassador Tina*

Taka and Tina strolled down the city streets that were well lit by the crystals installed on posts every twenty feet apart.

"What a wonderful night for a stroll," Tina said and took a deep breath. She exhaled with an 'Ah' sound.

Taka stayed silent as they walked. The events thus far were interesting and disturbing.

These students would be a challenge to teach. Some were prone to violence more than others and were dangerous.

Violet was one that would be the most challenging to keep track of since her guardian can teleport. He must be a dark fey. How else would he be explained? But it still did not explain why he would be. The Blythe hated mostly everyone even their own race. Could a human have that kind of magic? Unless he was a half-breed, and no one knew about it.

"Hey taka, you alright?" Tina asked in concern. Taka looked at her friend.

"Um... yes! I was just thinking is all," she replied.

"If you don't want to tag along. It's alright," Tina assured her.

"No. It's not that. I have been thinking about these students and their powers, magic. The Dark Princess is a great concern and Glen and Neola. They concern me also. They are human right. But we have never seen humans like them before. Where do they hail from and why have we not known what kingdom they are from?" Taka pushed.

"They are from here Taka," the ambassador said. Taka stopped in her tracks.

"What? How is that possible?" Taka said with doubt.

"I don't know Taka. Maybe the dragons have kept their kind hidden this whole time. Maybe, there is not many of them in the world," Tina suggested. Taka nodded in agreement. That was possible. The dragons did as they pleased. It was all because of them that all this was even possible to begin with. This school has taken generations of planning.

Soon, they were upon the next Ball party. They went inside and it was quite the sight. Mostly everyone was getting along here. Many people had coupled up and then some. They were told many had left to who knew where. Taka knew. This was all new for everyone. There would be a lot of sex and most likely pregnancies. This could be good and unbelievably bad at the same time.

Tina went and grabbed them drinks. Taka had a feeling they both would be roaring drunk when this night ended. Oh, well. They had two days to recover.

This party seemed tame and in order. Not much happening except a lot of mingling as it were. Taka rolled her eyes. She suddenly wanted to leave. But she stayed with her friend.

A couple hours later they left and went to the next student party. This one was a drag. Everybody that was still here were sitting around talking or doing nothing. It was a dull party.

They went to the fourth party and the place was doing well. People were dancing. Most were at the tables with food and drink. They were gambling and playing other games. This seemed good and they may do well in the school events to come later in the year.

It was getting really, late when they left for the last Ball party.

When they arrived, the place was almost empty. Almost two hours later everyone was gone but a single girl. She was all pink with white glyph like symbols on her. She sat there completely nude. Wait! She was a jelly creature. Taka had never seen one before. She did not know that one would be here.

The jelly girl was very humanoid like. No hair. She had extremely shapely curves. Huge, rounded breasts that jiggled when she stood up. Her bottom was large and round. Hips that would knock a man out. Thick lush curvy lips. Her eyes were dark almost a black.

"Hey sweetie," Tina said. "Where you from?" the ambassador asked.

The girl shrugged her shoulders.

"You know what dorm room you are in?" Taka asked.

"I not in school. But want to be," the jelly girl replied. Tina and Taka looked to each other.

"What should we do?" Taka asked. Tina smiled brightly.

"We enroll her in school of course," Tina said with flair and made a pose. Taka slapped her hand on her head.

"We have to leave anyhow. There is no one here. Party's over," Tina said.

So, they left. They went back the way they came. They still had to check in on the other parties again. This would go on until the Balls were over.

They walked inside the Ball Hall and it was empty. They were told everyone had left about an hour ago.

So, they went to the next which also happened to be empty and the next one was also. When they came to the next ball, the people were just leaving. That left only one more left.

When they got back to the very first party that started their night. Tina and Taka went inside and were shocked at how many people were still there. Over half had left but there were still hundreds more left. The two women groaned.

"Come on jelly girl. Let's go, party the night away," Taka said with irony. Tina rolled her eyes. The jelly girl nodded with a big smile.

Rose Encounter

The golden boy is intriguing!
-Rose

Neola had led Glen by the hand, out onto a terrace that went all around the whole building. She was in a sore mood. She kept the tears from her eyes the best she could.

They went to the rail that overlooked a manicured lawn. She then hugged him and hid her face. Glen held her close. She clung to him like she always did.

"I am sorry she treated you that way, my love," Glen whispered.

Someone cleared their throat.

"Excuse me. May we speak a moment please," A feminine voice spoke.

Glen and Neola were nearly startled out of their skins. They pulled away and looked at the woman and her guardian.

"Hello! My name is Rose," she said and stuck out her hand. Glen shook it.

"Glen," he introduced himself. Rose shook Neola's hand.

"Her name is Neola. She does not speak," Glen confirmed.

"Ah! I see," Rose said. "Well then. I wish to relay a message from me to you about my sister Violet, the Dark Princess. She has her sights on you, dear Glen. I suggest you take care. You as well Neola. For she despises you because of your affections for Glen. I, myself think you make a splendid couple," she affirmed her forewarning.

"Thank you, Mistress Rose, for your concern for our well being," Glen was sincere and bowed.

"My, so polite. Thank you, Lord Glen," rose said with a bittersweet smile.

"Well, I must be off. I have duties to perform," she concluded and walked away.

She had no idea why she wanted to warn the boy about her sister. Perhaps it was because she hated to see something unique go to waste, or that she had a heart after all.

Nah!

She was heartless. She loved nothing but her guardian and herself. Everything else was a means to an end.

Glen and Neola watched the woman walk away. Strange that a Blythe would be so considerate to warn them of danger. It was appreciated. Glen had already suspected Violet of plotting against whomever she thought was a threat. She did not try to hide the fact.

Glen held Neola's hand.

"Let's go," he said. Neola nodded and they left the party.

Trevor's Love Mates

What can I say?
I love women of all sorts!
-Trevor

Trevor and his dates tumbled into his dorm room with laughter all around. Been a long time since he felt this happy. He wondered if the same applied to the girls.

He locked his door as not to be disturbed by anyone. If there was a knock, he would just ignore them. He wanted all his attention on the girls. They deserved to be treated like queens.

He did wonder briefly as to where his sister had gone off to. He had not seen her since the tour. She was a lot like him. Always wandering off where she pleased. She should have been here to protect him from these women.

Oh, well, he thought in relief and joy. He hoped his sister was somewhere safe and is enjoying herself.

They all scrambled toward the bed. The goblin girl jumped up and down upon it and giggled. The other two women laughed.

"Hey Quorra. Purr haps Umay should go first," the feline woman suggested strongly.

"That is a great idea, Mischa," the orc woman replied. The goblin girl looked back and forth between the two.

"Really? I go first," she stuttered uncertainly.

"It will be fine. Right, Trevor," Quorra said huskily. The orc kissed the goblin's cheek. Then she gently removed the girl's hide skins from her body. Umay, the goblin girl's skin flushed a red tint that spread across her dark green flesh. Trevor looked on with longing. She was a petite girl of maybe five feet tall. Her green, black hair was down to the middle of her back. Her pointed ears could not hide in those locks. She had a firm tiny bottom and her apple sized breasts bobbed when they were released from her hides.

Quorra the orc woman removed her dress and it fell to the floor to show her creamy like greyish green flesh. Her breasts were small, muscled balls of joy. Her body muscled and smooth right to her bald pelvis. Trevor had never seen between a girl's thighs to have no hair before.

The feline girl undressed, and her large breasts bounced like they were full of milk.

Milk jugs, he thought lustfully. He gave his head a shake.

Umay laid down on the bed. She was on her back with her head at one side of the bed. Quorra held her friend's arms and spoke in a reassuring tone.

"I have never done this before," Umay said nervously. Umay looked to Trevor and her eyes went wide. Just as the orc girl's eye went wide.

"Oh, my," Quorra breathed.

A delightful purr escaped Mischa her tongue lulled out of her mouth.

"He is too big," the goblin cried out. "He will not fit," she stressed. Quorra hush her friend.

"It will be alright, Umay," Trevor said soothingly. "Just try to relax." He went to his knees on the floor. He brought his face to her triangle shaped patch of hair and kissed her pelvis. The girl was squeamish at first. Trevor went lower and his tongue lashed out along her dark greenish folds. Umay gasped. He licked gently and slowly to work her up and she in no time was wet and inviting. She moaned in pleasure.

The other girls watched in fascination. They had never heard or seen such a thing before. Then Mischa went under the bed and when she reached Trevor, she herself started to lick his manhood. He groaned pleasantly. Then her mouth went around, and she sucked hard. Trevor through his head back in pleasure. He then pulled away to Mischa disappointment.

Trevor reached on top of his nightstand and grabbed his cock sheath.

"What is that?" Quorra asked curiously.

"It is a cock sheath. It prevents a woman from getting pregnant during sex," he revealed.

"Really? How interesting," the orc mused thoughtfully.

It also protects you from me, he thought bitterly.

He rolled it on and made sure it fit nice. Then he lowered himself upon Umay. He rubbed the tip of his penis against her clit, and she responded by lifting her hips. His head slid in easily and he slow sunk in.

Umay cried out as a sharp pain hit her. Quorra consoled her.

"No worries. It will start to feel better soon. Trust me," the orc assured the goblin. Umay nodded.

"You smell good Quorra. Mm!" the goblin said. Her tongue lashed out and licked the orc's private area. Quorra was surprised at first, but she liked it in a guilty way. It felt nice and made her wet there.

Trevor just stayed where he was and let himself throb within her. Soon she began to feel better. No. Good. Trevor let Umay take control. Let her move the way she wanted. Her eyes closed as she convulsed spasmodically.

"Oh, Trevor. It feels so, good," she cried out loudly. He hips hit against Trevor hard and she keep crying his name.

Then Umay was panting out of breath.

"So, dizzy," she said tiredly.

Trevor pulled out of her slowly.

"Quorra. It was wonderful," the goblin said drowsily and passed out.

"My turn, purr," Mischa said as she rubbed up against Trevor and lean her ass up to him. Her tail swished about.

He placed himself behind the feline woman. She was dripping wet down her thighs. She was more then ready for him. Still, he entered her slowly and carefully. He was large and could hurt them if he were not careful.

The feline girl moved her hips into him. he controlled his pace and thrusted at a steadily. Mischa stretched out and clawed the bed as she shivered. Juices flowed out of her as her ecstasy overwhelmed her.

Trevor groaned deeply and pulled out. He removed the cock sheath, and he stroked his penis as he spurted out all over the feline girl's buttocks. She looked behind her to watch. She purred as the warm seed spilled on her.

Mischa purred as she rubbed her head against Trevor. He instinctively scratched behind one of her ears. She continued to purr.

"I like that," she said. She then went and curled up with Umay. Mischa's tail wrapped around them and she dozed.

Quorra had a disappointed look on her face suddenly.

"I guess you are finished," she asked with a frown.

"Far from it darlin," he said as he put his sheath back on. He grabbed the orc and shoved her down on the bed. She chuckled and bit her bottom lip. He was still large and hard and took charge. Quorra was even more excited than before. She wanted to feel his prowess. She lifted her legs behind her head and waited for him. She grinned.

"I like it a little rough," she confirmed.

He slipped inside her and slowly plunged all the way in. Quorra groaned huskily.

"Oh, Trevor. You are wonderful," she breathed in his ear.

"Not as wonderful as you ladies," he breathed back and kissed her mouth. He invaded and played with her tongue. The orc played back and teased and explored him.

Trevor was slow in his thrusts at first and then began to have a steady rhythm. He pumped Quorra's hips to her delight. She had an orgasm and then begged for him to drive into her harder and faster.

He obliged. Trevor fucked her with abandon. He slammed into her hard and fast.

"Oh, fuck Trevor you are so wonderful. More. More," she screamed out in her glory.

Trevor slammed into her and was so surprised that she could take his size inside her like this. She genuinely enjoyed his girth. To be able to fuck a girl like this was something he had never been able to do without ever hurting them. This orc, Quorra, was such a glorious woman to be with.

He pulled out as she begged him not to. He almost did not pull out. But he must. He pulled away the sheath and stroked his cock again. He squirted his seed onto her belly and breasts. There was so much like last time.

"Oh, my. There is so much," Quorra praised. I bet you could get at least ten women pregnant in a single shot," she bragged.

Trevor chuckled.

"I doubt that, but you never know," he said awkwardly. She eyed him.

"Can you go again, by chance?" she asked.

"Let's find out," he breathed into her mouth. His member grew hard again, and the sheath went back on.

Again, he entered inside the beautiful orc girl and they were brought to many heights of ecstasy.

When they were done, they panted and held one another close. Trevor enjoyed the feel of her.

"Will the three of you stay here with me until school starts?" he asked.

"I most definitely will. As, for them. Wait until morning to ask," she said and snuggle into his chest.

They soon fell asleep in each other's arms.

Finally, Over

Party like no tomorrow!
-Trevor

Taka and Tina were finally leaving the party. The sun had come up and began its blaze upon the city.

Tina staggered along with her friend and the jelly girl, who seemed bright eyed, and bushy tailed still. Taka wondered if her race slept at all. She sure hoped so. Taka was exhausted.

They were on their way to Tina's home. She lived in a house nearby. Taka had been there a few times. They were friends after all. Good thing they were going there. Tina's home had many rooms and Taka could use some sleep right now. She was glad that Tina's house was closer.

They made it and went inside. Tina went to the iron stove. She opened it up and sparked flames within. She filled water in a kettle from a tap, then put it on top of the stove. She grabbed three mugs off a shelf and put tea leaves in them.

"Tea will be ready soon. I will show you where you can sleep jelly girl," Tina said with a yawn. They followed her to a room that had a bed and dresser. There was a storage closet and a bathing room. The jelly girl went in and sat on the bed and smiled at them. Tina closed the door.

Tina walked down the hall and Taka followed.

"Tina I can find my own way to a guest room. We should get you to sleep," Taka said in concern.

"I be fine," Tina smiled. "I did not drink that much," she finished.

Taka knew that to be false. She sure felt like she had too many spirits. Taka led the ambassador to her own room anyway. Tina sat on the bed and Taka helped take her heels off.

Taka. You know how much I love you, right," Tina said. Taka blushed. She knew. This was not the first time they had this conversation. Tina wrapped her arms around Taka's neck. Tina kissed her friend and Taka kissed her back. Taka could never deny Tina anything. Tina pulled away.

"Maybe we cannot do this. With schooling and all," Tina said sadly.

"Well, school technically has not started yet," Taka reminded. Tina's eyes went bright.

"We have two days together then," the ambassador said.

The two women kissed with passion. A passion they have longed for many months now.

"Oh, Taka. Love me," Tina panted out. Taka did just that.

Sisterly rivalry

I wish my sisters would not fight all the time.
-*Poppy*

Rose went out of her way to find her sister Violet. It was time to put a thorn in her side, so to speak.

Her and Miles went back indoors and straight up the stairs to the second level.

Still there with Poppy.

She paused a moment. Poppy seemed upset about something. Violet was comforting her. Well, this was an interesting development. Did Violet really care for their sister?

Fascinating!

Rose walked over and leaned on the rail facing her sisters. She had a quirky smile that said she was up to no good.

Violet scowled at her.

"What do you want?" There was no sense in being polite with her words.

"Oh, my. Is that any way to greet your ever-loving sister?" Rose feigned being hurt.

Violet was not falling for her shit. She stepped in front of Poppy protectively. A snarl displayed her curled lip. Made her look more feral.

A glint shone from Rose's eye. She had struck a nerve.

"Poppy dear, are you alright? I am concerned about your welfare. Is there anything I could do for you?" Rose poured on the false bravado of caring for her sister.

Poppy stayed behind her sister Violet. Something did not feel right with Rose. She was a self-involved bitch but was well mannered and nice about some things. But this. This felt odd. Why would she pretend to care about her? It scared Poppy for some reason.

Violet gave a grin that spelled trouble would be on the way if one pushed too hard.

Rose on the other hand would not cross that line unless it was needed.

"Nice try liar, cunt, whore," Violet seethed and clenched her fists. She was spoiling for a fight. She wanted to show Rose how far she had come with her innate power. Her magic.

"If you ever need anything Poppy just come to me at anytime," Rose assured her.

"Fuck off!" Violet said with venom.

"Sister, there is no need for such hostilities. I am just concerned about my dear sisters," Rose quirked a grin.

"Get the FUCK away, you, sanctimonious cunt," Violet screamed. Energy surrounded Violet's fists and her eyes glowed.

"My apologies dear sister," Rose bowed. She turned and left with a quirked smile that soon spread wider. Now, all she had to do was pick at Violet each day so she could not concentrate in class.

"Time for us to go home, Miles," Rose said over her shoulder. "You still have a duty to perform, my love."

Observations

What a spectacle the party had been!
-Raymond

Raymond and his sister were on their way to the dorm rooms. They were the last two people to leave the party. Around the same time as Ambassador Tina and Doctor Taka.

"We have observed a lot of interesting events tonight. Do you not agree?" Raymond said with a lilt to his voice.

Raya rubbed her tired eyes and nodded.

"Yes brother. You were right all along about everything. I was surprised that those three women left with Trevor. But, maybe, it was not. He is charismatic after all, for a human that is," she threw in the last bit in hurriedly.

Almost, but she did say three women and not vile creatures like she used to in the past, Raymond thought with a smile.

"What else did you see, sister?" the elf prince asked.

"Glen and Neola left in a hurry. I think they may be a couple," Raya suggested.

"Yes. Could be. Or some sort of subterfuge," Raymond made his own suggestion.

Raya did not think so for some reason. She was sure that the two of them were lovers or will be. It was in the eyes. The way they looked at one another. She knew those types of looks. No one was capable of that kind of façade.

"What did you think of lady Violet?" Raymond asked.

"She is impetuous and dangerous, but so is her sister Rose, a conniving bitch. Poppy on the other hand is… what is the word I am looking for? Timid… and indecisive," Raya explained.

"Yes, indeed. She is also frightened of her sister Rose for some reason that she may not even know about. She is very fond of Violet and Violet of her," Raymond finished.

Raya thought about this. She agreed with her brother, but what if Poppy knew why she feared Rose. Just could not remember why because of trauma. She knew her brother was getting her to think about these events to come up with her own conclusions.

"Brother."

"Yes sister."

"I think the ambassador and the doctor are lovers," Raya said out of the blue. He stopped in his tracks and eyed his sister.

"What makes you think that?" he asked with interest. He wondered where she had come up with this. Did she see something he did not?

"Well, they seem to put up a good front. Tina does at lest. She gives no signs thus far except when we left. Anyway, Taka looks at her like a lover would. There is a yearning in her eyes. I see the eyes and can sense what these people desire. It is kind of strange," Raya finished.

"Well, dear sister. You have a talent I would like to exploit in the future. It might be helpful in finding out more about Glen and his guardian.," Raymond mused the last bit.

They continued to walk toward their dorm rooms. More talk about the party transpired. It was a hell of a time.

"I heard our party was the last to shut down and was the wildest. There were only a few fights. Many lovers were made last night also. How grand. Maybe there is hope for the races after all. I am willing to wager that Trevor shall have a fair share of women pregnant by school's year end," Raymond teased.

"Alright I will bite. I am willing to bet that Glen and Neola are engaged to be married and are from two different houses. I say this because of the crests they wear. There is something special about them!" Raya was certain about it. Raymond agreed. But why did he have this feeling of dread?

"So, Raya. Has anyone caught your eye?" Raymond was curious. He observed his sister carefully and she did take an interest in someone, but he had not figured it out, yet.

"Not really. There are some interesting people and yes men. I have to admit that the other races may not be so bad after all," Raya was reluctd to confess.

"So, there is someone of interest," Raymond smiled.

"There might be a few, brother and it is none of your business," she said and stuck her tongue out at him.

There were two people she wished to be with but did not believe it was possible. She was not going to reveal that to her brother.

There was more talk and ideas thrown about and what their thoughts were about the first official day of school.

Rose Loves

I only love Miles!
-*Rose*

They entered the dorm room. Rose was in a particularly good mood and showed it. She walked to her desk and poured a glass of wine. She then handed it to her guardian.

"Drink up. It is time to celebrate, my love," Rose said haughtily.

He drank the glass in a single gulp. She looked at him. He moved to her. He had left some wine in his mouth. He knew what she liked, and she like her wine straight from his mouth. He kissed her and the wine spilled into her mouth. She drank it and her tongue played with Miles'. He moaned into her mouth and she moaned back.

She then pulled away. The glint in her eye meant something naughty was on her mind.

"I want you to rip this dress from my body and ravage me. Fuck me like no tomorrow, my love," she commanded.

"Yes, my Queen," Miles said heatedly.

He did as she commanded. He tore the dress from her. She gave a laugh of excitement. He grabbed her roughly but gently at the same time. His mouth went to her breast and he sucked on a nipple hard. It made her feel good. She panted. Miles lifted her one leg and plunged himself it quick and hard. He gyrated his hips fast with demand. In no time at all Rose reached her peak and loudly moaned her pleasure.

Miles picked her up and dropped her on the bed and she giggled.

"Oh, yes Miles. Fuck me hard, my love," she taunted.

He grabbed onto her legs and thrusted into her like a battering ram. Rose threw her head up.

"Oh, yes. You know how I like it. You are my one and only," she roared. He jammed into her and kept slamming his hips. Miles got her off many times.

She moved out from him and turned around. He began to slip into her again as she lifted her ass up to him.

"No Miles," she said. She turned to look at him seductively. "The other hole. I want to try something naughtier tonight. Fuck me good, my love," she begged.

Miles slid into her and let out a groan of pleasure. Rose gasped in lustfulness. He pumped a few times and Rose begged him.

"Miles, spill in me as I release, oh," she rasped some more.

He released on her command. He spilled his love into his queen.

"Oh, my Queen," he growled in pleasure.

What a glorious fuck, Rose thought with a grin of satisfaction.

They curled up together in the bed. She held him to her breast. He sucked on her breast.

"Yes, my love. Suckle away. Mm! Feels so good," she moaned out. She would climax again soon.

"Tomorrow, my love. You must spill your seed within me to make a baby. We need our heir to the throne. You are my Regent!" she stated. "Our empire awaits us."

She then had her climax. Her guardian then fell asleep as she stroked his hair. Then she too went to sleep. Her dreams were of him as they ruled on high. A throne shared together with their children at their feet.

Somewhere in the Past

Praise the warriors who fight for freedom;
Praise the battles that are won in their name.
Hail the warriors for their valor;
Hail the battles never lost.
-*Chimera's Lay*

Wondering the ruins, they were in awe of the massive structures still standing. Who were these people that lived here and where did they go? It was a question that may never be answered.

Krawlin knew, but he said nothing. Nor would he. This was a mystery left alone. The humans with him knew nothing of the past here, and it would stay that way.

He was here on orders from the council of Tulladiss. He was here to bring something back. Problem was where to find this treasure as in were.

This was a huge city. There was no city this large in world. To walk through this city would take days. Not that it mattered. Krawlin had the time, but these humans had such short life spans.

Time to get to work. The artifact had to be found. If he had to search every single building he would. So, he just chose a random building and went from there. The building he chose would haunt him for many years to come as so many lives died searching within.

What Krawlin did not know was that he and his crew were being watched.

Princess Catrice

I have my own plans for Glen!
-*Princess Catrice*

Princess Catrice and her guardian Gianna marched down the hallway right to Neola's Door. Gianna knocked firmly.

"Neola, are you in?" Catrice called out. There was no answer. The princess sighed. She nodded to Gianna. The guardian opened the door, and they went inside. It was dark and empty. Neola was not there. The princess stood there in the dark for a moment thinking. Then she turned and left.

She then went to Glen's door. There Gianna gave a firm knock and waited.

"Glen. Are you in?" the princess asked. She narrowed her brows and nodded. Gianna opened the door. Catrice walked into another empty dark room. Again, she stood for a few moments. This time with clenched fists. She huffed and stalked out of the room. The princess grabbed Gianna's hand and tugged her along to their dorm room.

When they got in the room Catrice slammed the door shut.

"Oh, how could they?" the princess screamed. She went to the bed picked up a pillow and threw it across the room.

Gianna stood there and waited for her princess to calm down her temper tantrum.

Catrice took her rings off her fingers and threw them to the floor. She took away her bracelets and they too ended being thrown to the floor. She took her dress off and everything. All upon the floor.

"Where are they at? Do they not know that it could be dangerous out there?" the princess stressed. She paced around the room.

She stopped and looked at Gianna surprised.

"Why are you not undressed yet?" Catrice demanded.

Gianna blinked.

"Princess?" she questioned.

Catrice strode right to Gianna. The princess started to help the woman undress.

"Princess. Must we do this now?" Gianna fussed.

"Yes! You will please me! I need release Gianna," Catrice spurned. "Take your damn clothes off and fuck me already," she gritted and pushed her guardian on the bed. Gianna's clothes were removed and Catrice came in close. Her finger touched Gianna's lips.

"I wish I had a body like yours, Gianna. All muscle, textured, strong," Catrice's voice grew husky. She slid two of her fingers inside Gianna's love space. The guardian moaned.

"So, wet and inviting for me. So, smooth inside. So, strong. I bet you could crush a man's cock in here," the princess breathed. Gianna moaned and moaned. Begged. She gyrated her hips.

Catrice' fingers worked their magic as they moved about inside the warmth of Gianna's womanhood.

"Oh, princess. Please princess. Give me release. Oh, princess," Gianna moaned her release and bucked her hips.

Princess Catrice laid down on the bed and Gianna climbed on top of her.

"Gianna. Love me like I love you," she pleaded. Gianna kissed her hard.

"Always my Princess."

Jelly Girl

I would like to study her!
-Doctor Taka

She was bored. She needed to find something to do. She did not sleep, for she did not know what sleep was or require it. She was a Jelly Girl. Sometimes referred as a slime.

Here she was in someone's home with nothing to do. Well, this slime girl was about to go somewhere fun.

She went through the house. She heard weird noises coming from one of the bedrooms but ignore it. She saw that the kettle was boiling on the stove and that there were tea mugs. So, she made herself a tea. She tasted the brew and found it quite good.

She then walked outside into the bright sunlight. She has never been in such a place before. It was exciting to be here.

What was school anyway? She mused this over as she wandered the streets. People stared at her as more folks went about their daily routines.

Jelly girl, sometime 'slime', enjoyed the sights seen and the multitude of peoples that were about. In her travels she has seen only separated peoples. Never any diversity.

All her years alive there was always war and strife. This city on the other hand was different. People worked together here. In a peaceful manner no less.

She decided she liked it here and wanted to stay for a while. Get to know people. Although they did seem leery of her. She was vastly different and an unknown. Most peoples of the world had no clue as to what she was. Guess that was what the school would teach, right!

She walked down an alley that was darkened with shadow. She marveled that there were so many routes that led everywhere around the city. Roads with sidewalks. So many buildings tucked together.

Then she met a cloaked and hooded person. She waved her hand in greeting.

The figure pulled a blade out.

"Die you freak," he growled and thrusted his blade under her one breast. The jelly girl gasped and melted herself into a puddle.

The man was taken aback and moved away.

"What the…" he blurted out.

The puddle bubbled, then a giant fist hit him in the middle section and the man flew over the next building across the way.

"Oops! My bad!" the jelly girl said with a cringe. She did not suspect she would have hit him that hard.

She reformed to her girl figure and walked on. She totally forgotten about the incident. Where was she to go, now?

Lovers at Last

"Glen loves!"
-Neola

Sneaking into his dorm room, Glen let out a breath of relief. He locked his door and went to his window. He unlatched it, opened it, and waited.

In no time Neola was there and she leaped into his arms. She was all smiles and giggles. To hear her utter a sound brought joy to Glen.

Neola was still in her dress. She still bore her golden self also. Her silver eyes smiled up at him. Then they turned purple, her normal colour. Those eyes enchanted him.

They moved and had a hint of change behind them. He could she the many forms they would take. Glen touched her cheek, and she began to change back. Her golden skin got replaced by her purple flesh and the pale three lavender stripes returned to her cheeks. Her purple lips pierced, Glen leaned in and kissed them softly. Her tongue spread his mouth apart so she could make her way in and tease his.

She started to undo the buttons of his tunic. It was removed and fell to the floor. She untied his shirt with deft fingers. He then pulled his shirt over his head and it too landed on the floor. Glen's breathing quickened.

Neola's eyes locked on his as she started to undo his breaches. His loins stirred. His body became heated, and his skin flushed. His breaches dropped to the floor and he stepped away from them.

Neola licked her lips and took him in. She touched his chest and traced her fingers down his rippling muscles to the abs. She stopped there and watched as his member grew and throbbed. Her eyes were wide. She loved every part she saw of him.

Glen touched her chin. His eyes were glassy with tears.

"Neola. I am frightened of not being able to please you. I do not know what must be done. I have never done this before," he confessed with a frown. His anxiety was getting the best of him.

Neola gently touched his cheek.

"Glen loves. Neola loves. Together!" she stated.

She gently pushed on his chest and led him to the bed. Once the back of his legs bumped into the edge, he sat down. She stood before him and he tenderly removed the straps of her dress from her arms. The dress slipped down to the floor to reveal Neola in all her glory. Her averaged sized breasts perked up. Her hard erect nipples were purple almost a black in colour. Her smooth hard muscled body curved smoothly and gently with a roundness that showed how delicate she could be. There was a small strip of hair on her pelvis. Lavender lines started from her hips and wrapped around down around her ass cheeks as she slowly turned around for Glen's viewing pleasure. She had a gap between her thighs that showed her womanly sights.

Neola leaned into Glen. He laid back as she climbed on top of him. She gripped his strong pulsing manhood in her small hand. She carefully brought him to the entrance of her womanhood. Slowly he went into her wetness. She was warm and inviting that Glen groaned in passion. She leaned in and their lips met in a deep kiss. Then Neola forced her hips down upon him. They both winced and gasped as a sharp pain hit them. Glen felt the fold of his skin pull back tightly and it felt like it tore open, but he felt pleasure afterward.

Neola felt something similar as she was broken open. A tearing of flesh inside.

They both bled and it leaked upon Glen's pelvis and thighs.

Tears sparked in Neola's eyes. Glen embraced her.

"I am sorry…" Neola's finger hushed him, and she shook her.

"No, sorry. Feels good, now," she said.

"I love you, Neola," Glen breathed. He put his mouth to one of her breasts and sucked a nipple gently. His touches were tender and flamed Neola's body into action. She moved her hips slowly, feeling the pulse of his penis within her. Something was building within and when it reached its breaking point… Neola thrusted her head back and moaned loudly.

"Oh, Glen," she rasped. Her insides convulsed around Glen and he groan her name continuously and release inside her. She felt it and ecstasy hit her again. She clung to him and Glen held her ever close.

The pleasure had hit them so quickly that they barely knew what happen. It happened so fast.

They panted into each other's mouth. Glen loved Neola's lips upon his. They kissed so deeply, and they would not stop. This felt so right. They loved.

Glen still pulsed and Neola still stayed on him.

"Glen, more," she panted.

He would do anything for her. Her pleasure was infectious, and he felt himself on the verge again. Somehow, she knew he would erupt again. He grabbed her firm ass and exploded inside her again. It seemed that the pleasure Neola felt was continuous. She kept flexing around Glen. Her muscles were so strong and excited him.

Glen found himself not wanting to stop. It felt too wonderful that he just had to please Neola some more. To give her all of him.

"Glen loves," Neola panted and moaned. Her orgasms kept shivering throughout her body. Energy emanated from her like threads. Glens threads of life reached out to her. Their threads intertwined and fused as one. They were becoming one soul. This was a marriage of two souls of eternal love.

Their heights of pleasure had risen beyond what they could comprehend. They roared their pleasure, and the dorm rooms shook and rumbled but a brief instant.

There was a bright flash of a silvery purple light, then was gone.

Neola collapsed upon Glen. Both had heavy breathing. Sweat drenched their bodies and soaked the bed. They were too tired too doing anything but lie in each other's arms.

Glen grabbed the blanket and covered them with it.

"Neola," Glen whispered her name in such a tender tone that it could barely be heard. Neola smiled.

"Glen," she whispered back with loving emotion.

They were two souls' content and happy.

Sneaky Kitty

Purrfect!
-Mischa

Mischa was awake and up to some mischief. She swished her tail about. She was using magic and kept it subtle as possible.

She could see well in the dark. Her cat eyes opened wide, and the pupils swallowed the iris. She purred soothingly. Quorra slept soundly and Trevor slept. Mischa weaved her magic to keep them asleep while she followed through with her plan. She was a curious kitten after all.

She licked the goblin girl's face.

"Wake up, Umay," the feline whispered in her ear. She stirred but stayed asleep. Mischa smiled at an idea that formed in her mind. She lulled her tongue out again and licked between the girl's thighs. She licked until the goblin awoke. She moaned softly.

Umay opened her eyes and rubbed them. She was tired and groggy.

"We have to be quiet, alright," Mischa said quietly. The goblin girl nodded.

"Look Umay. Trevor is ready for you again," the feline kept her voice lowered and pointed. Umay looked in the direction pointed and saw that Trevor was indeed hard and ready again.

"Go. Climb on top," Mischa urged. "You said you wanted to have his baby, right," Mischa coaxed. Umay nodded.

"You think it will be alright, even though he is asleep?" the goblin questioned.

"Of course, it will. It will be a surprise for him. So, let's just keep this between us, alright," Mischa smiled. Umay agreed.

Umay made her way over to Trevor and mounted him. A whimper escaped her.

"Shush, Umay. Our secret, remember," the feline held her hand over the goblin girl's mouth.

Mischa tail stayed in motion the whole time weaving her spell.

Umay moved her hips and she groaned through the feline's hand. Her climax came quickly and so did Trevor's. His seed fill the goblin girl and she just about screamed which almost woke him.

Umay moved away and Mischa sent her to the bathing room. The feline woman grabbed a rag, wet it down and cleaned Trevor up. She then went into the bathing room to join the goblin girl.

Mischa came into the water with a purring smile. She went up to Umay, close.

"What are you doing?" Umay said uncomfortably. Mischa looked at her seductively with lowered eyes.

"Wanting to be intimate with you," Mischa purred and kissed Umay. The goblin girl shivered in both pleasure and uncertainty.

Umay gave in and kissed the feline back. She felt Mischa place two fingers inside her and massaged her gently.

"Here, I will show you how," Mischa said. The goblin place two of her fingers inside the feline girl. She took care and was slow. Mischa purred in delight as Umay got the hang of it and explored.

The two girls brought each other to climatic heights.

They washed up and felt a rumble. They looked at each other perplexed. But nothing else happened for a long while.

Later, they went back into the bed. Umay climbed in with her back against Trevor and Mischa laid down facing Umay. They embraced one another with Trevor's arm around them.

Soon, they were sound asleep with a sneaky kitty purring happily.

Day of Rest

Get all the rest you need.
School starts soon.
-Ambassador Tina

Groggy with both sleep and a hangover, Taka opened her eyes. The brightness of sunlight hurt, and she groaned miserably.

Tina rolled over and draped her arm around the doctor. Taka could not help but smile. Tina then snuggled closer. The doctor held her friend and lover. She kissed the Ambassador's head. Taka loved her friend very much, but they could not have a true relationship. They both wanted to have a husband one day and a family. Taka sighed.

She wished she could have a husband and her friend, and both have children. Why not have the same husband? Taka could handle that. She would prefer that. She honestly thought about talking to Tina about it.

She just lied there with her eyes closed and dozed. Content being with her friend and sharing this time together.

Taka laid there until Tina roused herself from sleep. She gave a weak grin and rubbed her eyes. She blinked many times before they were able to stay open as slits.

The ambassador kissed Taka softly.

"Good morning?" she questioned. "Or is it close to being evening?" she jested.

Taka stood up and stretched.

"I will make us something to eat. Then my dear it shall be bath time," Taka said and yawned. She was thirsty. A nice cold glass of water would be great right now.

"I cannot wait until our bath, dear," Tina teased. Taka slapped her own bare ass as she walked away.

"A fine ass you have, my love," Tina whispered to herself sadly.

She curled her knees up on the bed and leaned on them. She wondered if her and Taka could ever be a couple? Not with these rules in place. She sighed. She aspired to having a husband and children one day. Where would that leave her dear friend? She frowned. She hated the thought of Taka never being in her life. They loved each other. There had to be a way.

Soon, the smell of food cooking caught her attention. Out of bed. She walked down the hall and checked in on the jelly girl. She was not in her room. Tina let out a breath.

Where the heck did the jelly girl go? She thought. She left the room and joined Taka in the kitchen.

"The jelly girl is gone," Tina said in a bored tired tone.

"Perhaps, she will come back. We could go look for her later if you like," Taka suggested.

"No, thanks. Rather stay here with you, my love," Tina replied.

Taka sensed something in her friend's tone. She sounded down suddenly. Why? The doctor became concerned. Well, they would talk while having a bath. Time enough to worry later.

The strips of meat were finished cooking and she put them on a plate.

She then cracked six eggs and they fried until they turned white and flipped them one by one. The bread toasted nicely when buttered when put on a grill.

She sliced some goat cheese. Had a tray with glasses of chilled milk, water with ice, two shots of spirits, and a jug of chilled berry juice.

Taka then sliced up an apple and a pear. She added green peas and carrots. Eggs were hot and ready on the plate now.

"Grab the tray of drinks please, my dear," Taka asked politely as she carried the large oval plate away.

"Hey. Where are you going?" Tina asked as she grabbed the tray and followed her friend down the hall.

Taka went into the bathing room and set the plate down near the end. She loved to be able to walk around nude with no worries.

Tina followed her lead and sat her tray down next to the plate.

"Come on in," Taka said as she went into the water. Tina went in and Taka kissed her briefly. The doctor grabbed a piece of fruit and placed it in the ambassador's mouth.

"I love you, Tina," Taka said looking into her friend's eyes longingly.

"I love you too," Tina responded while chewing with her hand over her mouth.

"Tina. I want to talk about something important and I hope we can find a way to make this work," Taka said. Tina nodded as Taka put a strip of meat in her mouth. Tina took a drink of milk which left her with a mustache.

Taka giggled and wiped her friend's face.

"I... I want to be with you. Maybe find the same husband and have a family together," she said slowly and awkwardly. Tina's eyes bulged out. She had never heard of such a thing before.

Taka did not like the look on her friend's face. She was sure that she had said something wrong. That she went too far.

"That would be wonderful Taka," Tina shouted and hugged her friend.

"We could raise our children here in this house. We could live together. Oh. What a great idea," Tina said excitedly. "Oh, I knew you were smarter than me," Tina praised.

"I would not go that far…" Taka tried.

"Taka," Tina said with a heavy voice.

"Yes!"

"Please stay another night and make love to me."

They kissed then. There emotions laid bare to one another.

Outing

Always respect women with love and affection and treat them to dinner, shopping, and the attention they deserve!
-Trevor

When morning came, Trevor and the girls awoke and bathed together. Trevor in no time started his usual horseplay. Soon, everyone was splashing and carrying on in laughter. Screams of joy could be heard and Trevor felt happy. He was happy being with these girls. He liked them. He wanted to spend time with them. This was not his usual lay them and leave them kind of deal.

Trevor was dunked under the water many times. Then he would raise up and splash water everywhere and the girls would screech in laughter.

There were sneaky kisses that they all found time for when playing. Trevor enjoyed slapping their fine asses. Umay enjoyed a little too much. She eventually climaxed while everyone teamed up on her.

"Someone likes it freaky," Mischa purred in the goblin's ear. Umay blushed.

"I cannot help it. It feels nice," she said with guilt.

"Meow! No need to feel guilty. I like to be spanked too," Mischa revealed with a wink. The feline produced her bottom to the goblin girl.

"Go ahead. Slap my bottom," Mischa purred. Umay did. She gave it a good hard slap and giggled.

Mischa then ravaged the goblin girl's mouth with her own. They touched each other until climax. Trevor and Quorra watched with interest and smiled.

"Well, that was exciting. Who wants to eat now? Let's all go out and then I will take you ladies shopping," he said with all the charm of a man who kept his promises.

To put up with me, they deserve to be treated like princesses. They are so beautiful, Trevor thought. He has grown fond of them in such a short time. He smiled wolfishly. He was going to continue to have fun with them for as long as it takes.

He dressed and waited for the girls to finish their goings on. Quorra put her dress back on. She was gorgeous.

"I find that you are more beautiful without the dress," Trevor said with a wolfish grin. Quorra giggled.

"You are a tease. Mm! I like it very much," she said, and her lips brushed his. Trevor loved the feel of her lips and her body against his.

The other two girls came out dressed and ready at last. They kept pawing each other. The Dhyme Lord thought it cute.

"We go out to eat then get you girls some new clothes and I think each of you should chose where you want to shop," he said.

All three girls hugged him.

"Thank you!" they said in unison.

They left to spend the day together out in the city.

They went to a nearby restaurant to eat. Trevor and the girls ordered all the food that they liked. They ate well. There was talk about what to do next.

Soon, they went to a clothing shop and Trevor bought a lot of clothing for them. There were two bags each. Surprisingly, they did not spend much time there. It was like the girls knew what they wanted and just got it.

"So, Umay. Where would you like to shop next," Trevor asked her. She whispered it in his ear.

"Really?" he asked. "Alright then. Let's go," he said loudly.

When they reached their new destination Umay was in her glory. The shop they were in was full of toys. Who knew that a goblin liked toys so much?

Umay chose three toys. A stuffed wolf, a human porcelain doll, and a puzzle box. Interesting choices, indeed.

Umay thanked Trevor with a kiss and then seemed preoccupied with her toys.

Mischa wanted to go to a jeweler. Just as the old stories spoke of. Cats like shiny things.

Mischa chose a ring. It was simple enough. Silver with an engraved pattern. It was the only thing she wanted.

Trevor noticed that the shop keepers were polite and accommodating. They never gave strange looks or treated him or the girls badly. They were friendly.

Next stop was Quorra's favorite place to go. It was a weapons shop. Trevor somehow should have known.

The orc girl picked out an axe. It was a lethal looking thing with a broad blade that thinned out to a point. Done deal. It was hers.

It was not even midday yet and they had done so much. They went back to his dorm room. The girls tried on their new clothes. They teased each other and taunted one another. They carried on and laughed.

Trevor watched them and admired their interactions. When he first met them, it was about sex, but now, he wanted their companionship, to hang out with them. They were fun to be around.

The sex was great too. Tonight, would be a fun night yet again. Trevor gave his wolfish smile. It was time for him to join in on the fun.

Poppy is Grumpy

I really like him sis!
-*Poppy*

Poppy and Violet were out on the town this fine sunny morning. Violet was taking her sister out for breakfast.

They ordered their food and ate. They talked about the party the night before. Then when they finished their food. Trevor had come in with his three girlfriends. Poppy's mood went from smiling and chatting to her sister to dower and dull. They left without hesitation. Violet decided to take her sister shopping. Maybe that would cheer her up a bit. It did work. They looked over the sweets stands in the streets and Poppy sure liked her candy food.

Violet bought a bag of them. There were hard shelled candies with a soft center. Some were hard coated candy on a stick, they were called Jolly Pops. Those were her favorite kind.

They walked along and Poppy's mood improved, and she began humming. But later her hum changed as she saw Trevor and his girls in the clothing shop. Poppy turned her head away and ignored him.

Good girl, sis, Violet thought with a smirk.

They moved on and cut down another street. Poppy pointed to a shop. Violet smiled. She had not seen toys in such a long time. In they went. Poppy grabbed a stuffed bunny and a doll that looking eerily like her.

She went to the counter to pay when she saw Trevor with the other girls. Poppy frowned and a groaned escaped her lips. Violet's brows narrowed. When they left Violet, and Poppy went and paid for their items.

Violet had gotten a stuffed werewolf and handed it to Poppy.

"I know how you like these creatures. I thought you would like it," Violet said.

Poppy had tears in her eyes. She hugged her sister and cried.

"Thank you, Violet. Thank you for being my sister. I love you," Poppy sputtered.
Violet hugged her back. She was going to make this a good day for Poppy.

They continued their walk and came to the jewelry shop and again they ran into Trevor and his girls.

Fuck this shit, Violet thought in annoyance. They left the sight of the shop. Strolled down another street. They were nearing a weapons shop when Violet noticed Trevor and those girls go in. Poppy had not noticed.

"Know what sis?" Violet said. "I have an idea. I am going to get you some new clothes for school. That way you can look impressive. If you catch my meaning," Violet hinted. Poppy nodded and off they went.

Clothes were purchased and jewelry bought. Violet even picked up some make up. She would have her sister looking so good during school, it would get, not just Trevor's attention, but all the other boys too.

Rose Watches

I spy with my little eye;
My sister Violet,
As I watch her die.
-*Rose*

To be out and about with Miles was nice. Rose planned on buying him a gift or maybe two. He deserved it after all. Her lovely man that would bring her many children.

Question is, what to buy him? He was not into much really, unless it was between her thighs that is. She smiled. Get him a new suit for dinner tonight. She felt deep down that if she were to end up pregnant, that would more than satisfy him.

They went into a clothing shop. Miles was measured and Rose had specs for the tailor. She would have a special suit made for him. He had his stoic look when in public. This was why she preferred him in the bedroom. The looks he gave her brought excitement.

She sure hoped schooling did not interfere with their baby making, because that would not do.

They left when finished in the shop. They browsed the wares in the streets and shops. Rose noticed her two sisters out and about. Her and Miles followed them for a little while. Rose found it interesting how those two got along. It seemed Poppy had affections for that Trevor fellow.

Rose observed them for a time before she lost interest and she took Mile out for food. They ate and she spoke about her sisters. Wondering how those two became close. None of them were close out of all sisters in the family except the twins of course. Those two were horrible children. Always playing pranks on everyone. You could not tell them apart. It was annoying.

Rose stirred her food with a bored expression. She let out a little sigh.

"Miles. I would like to…" she paused as her eyes widened. Her mouth dropped.

No way! He would never dare. Would he? Please tell me he is daring, Rose thought as butterflies fluttered in her belly. Her cheeks grew hot as they flushed a rosy colour.

"My Queen. Will you marry me," he asked as he held the most beautiful ring with a stone she had never seen before. It was a deep red and cut like her name's sake.

It is a fucking rose ring, she observed. Rose looked at Miles with tears.

"Of course, I will you, big lug of a man," she praised him. "You are the most wonderful man ever," she continued her praise.

She stood up and walked around the table to sit in his lap. Her lips met his in a deep loving kiss that lasted an extremely long time.

"We must go find a place to get married right away, today," Rose said in determination.

They left and went around the city. Rose asked if there was such a place where marriages were arranged, and she was led to the administration building.

There they signed into a register book and were given a certificate. Rose was impressed with how thorough it was recorded.

It was a small ceremony to mark their spiritual union. The mister of weddings blessed them, and they kissed to seal the deal.

They left in a hurry. Rose was excited to get back to the dorm rooms to make a baby.

It was the most wonderous sex she had ever experienced, and she was damn sure a baby was pumped into her.

Rose laid there with a serene smile. Content to be in the arms of the man she loved.

Jelly Girl Again

Me slime!
-Jelly Girl

The jelly-slime girl still roamed about in the streets of the city. She was not lost. She knew her way back. She just enjoyed exploring like she always has.

She watched people and how they interacted. She could mold her body and form it to what ever shape she wished. She could fit through the smallest spaces and hide. She followed some people. Two girls that were sisters went shopping. They got along and supported each other. They were family. Jelly wished she had family.

She had no idea about her own kind. Where they were or from. She just called herself a jelly or slime because that was what she resembled. She had no name. She learned to speak and change from everything she observed.

She saw another woman and a man she was with follow the two sisters. The lady seemed interested in what the other girls were doing. Thing is those girls kept running into that Trevor boy and his friends.

Jelly girl stopped observing them and moved on elsewhere. She as other people interacted and shopped around in shops and at the street stands.

She grabbed an apple and ate it. No one noticed her take it. She liked the taste of foods and the different drinks. She did not know or understand that she was stealing. But every so often she would grab food to eat.

Jelly-slime girl was not some kind of pudding creature that was see through. She was a solid pliable creature that could take on any shape and mimic liquid like substance even though she was not. She could not shape change into anyone, no. She would always be the same colour and texture she was. She was a pink colour with white textured marks around her breasts, thighs, ass, calves, arms, and forehead.

People began to stare at her. Not because she was different, which may have been in part, but that she walked the streets nude. Not a care in the world this girl. The concept of wearing clothes was lost on her.

She did however notice she was being observed and thought that she should leave. She went to another part of the city. It was time to find something else to do.

Another Morning

I want a family with Taka!
-Ambassador Tina

Taka awoke again in Tina's bed. She stretched with a smile on her face. She would enjoy this moment. Tomorrow was the first official day of school. The doctor breathed out a small sigh.

She got out of bed and went to the kitchen. She put wood in the stove and snapped her fingers. A fire ignited and soon the stove grew warm. Filling the kettle with water it was placed on the stove and two mugs of tea were prepared.

Taka yawned and went back to the bedroom to wake her friend. She leaned down and kissed her friend till she woke. Tina smiled tiredly.

"Morning, my love," she yawned and stretched. "Are we going to shop for a husband today?" Tina joked and laughed at the expression on her friend's face.

"Tina. You are incorrigible," Taka fainted shock.

The two women kissed.

"Taka. Will you stay another night, please?" Tina begged.

Taka wanted to say no. She had to get ready for tomorrow, yet she could not deny her friend. Taka wanted another night with her, to love her. It would be a long time before they could be together again.

"Yes! I will stay, but I must go home first and get a few things like my teacher's clothes for tomorrow," Taka stressed playful and wagged her finger.

Tina grew excited and jumped up. She hugged Taka.

"Thank you so much. I love you," Tina said happily. "You are the best." Their kiss lingered awhile before they went into the kitchen for tea.

"So, Taka maybe during the school year we might find a husband. Like maybe a fellow professor, or even one of the students," Tina suggested.

Taka gasped with her hand over her mouth. She could not believe her friend had just said that about a student.

"Tina. How could you. They are too young for the likes of us," Taka reprimanded.

"What about Glen? He is yummy looking. I would so ride him like a pony," Tina giggled like a schoolgirl herself.

Taka's mouth dropped.

"You would not dare," Taka said shocked.

"Of course, I would. He is hot and would be perfect for us. Young, strong, vital, and could pump a ton of babies into us," Tina said with a glint in her eye. "Not like there is such a thing as 'age of consent'," Tina laughed with a 'HA'.

"Well, we have to abide by the rules of the school, and I am going to bring up the age of consent thing to the administration and say it was your idea," Taka said sternly.

Tina gasped. Her eyes went wide.

"You would not dare," Tina said in a low growly voice.

"I would, and what are you going to do about it," Taka teased.

"I going to punish you all day and night in the bedroom," the ambassador said and kissed Taka's mouth.

"After we get your things from home. you are in my bed until mourning," Tina breathed.

"I would not have it any other way," Taka breathed back.

Spending Time Together

> Shift to hide;
> Shift to fight.
> Shift to blend;
> Shift to assassinate!
> -*Changeling verse*

Neola awoke for the second time in Glen's bed, and she was happy and content. She snuggled in closer to her man. Glen, the love of her life. She knew him as he knew her. They were a well-kept secret that no other in the world knew about.

What had happened to their memories? Why could she not remember where she was from. What about Glen. He had no memories and knew nothing of where he was from. Neola was sure they came from the same place. It was just a feeling. It felt to them that they had known each other their whole lives.

Neola felt so alive with him. Their love making was unlike anything she could have ever imagined. They were bonded spiritually now. They had shaken the earth.

Glen opened his eyes and smiled. He kissed her lips tenderly. Her mouth opened and his tongue went in to explore her. Neola wanted to be explored and she wanted to explore him.

There was a knock at the door. They froze in place.

"Glen. Can we talk?" It was Princess Catrice. "Please. Neola is not answering her door, and I… want to apologize to her." She went silent.

"We can talk tomorrow at school, princess," Glen said annoyed. He really did not want to speak to her now.

"Alright," her voice muttered.

Glen and Neola waited a few minutes. Then Neola got out of bed. She gripped Glen by the hand.

"Glen. Bath," she said with a grin. Glen smiled back. They went into the bathing room. They would spend this time together. School would keep them busy for a while. Glen did not look forward to being away from Neola one bit. Perhaps they could sneak away at times. He looked forward to trying.

They washed each other and fondled one another. Soon, they were back in bed. Love making their little hearts out.

Rejected

What am I to do, Gianna?
-Princess Catrice

Her hand rested on the door after Glen had rejected to speak with her. Catrice was upset with him and Neola. This sort of thing has never happed before. What had gotten into her at the party to say such things to Neola?

She sighed and left to go back to her room. She hoped everything would be better tomorrow.

She walked into her room. Gianna frowned and hugged the princess.

"I wish they would speak to me," Catrice whined.

"There, there, Princess. They will come around. You will see," Gianna assured her.

"What if the earthshaking was because of him. What if…"

"Princess. He does not have that kind of power. These mountains have tremors at times," Gianna said.

"I do not know. It felt different," Catrice mused.

"Well, I am not feeling bad all day. So, Gianna you will stay here in my bed for the day and make me happy," Catrice demanded.

"Yes, princess," Gianna said with a smile and climbed back into bed.

As Catrice climbed into bed with her guardian. She thought about the small earth shake. She was still suspicious and would find out at some point as to its cause.

Then their lips were kissing, touching, and moans of pleasure escaped their hot moist mouths.

Orenda

I must protect my brother!
The very thing that gets him into trouble;
Shall be what keeps him out of trouble!
-Orenda

Orenda, Trevor's older sister, spoke with the three girls on the terrace. She told them that Trevor would be out here shortly and would notice them. They grew excited by this prospect.

What nobody else knew was that Orenda and Mischa have known each other for some years now. The Dhyme were not like other nations. They were more than human. They did not have the same hatreds as the other humans. They wanted to know other races and be apart of the world like they always have.

So, Mischa and Orenda had a meeting together and came up with a plan to keep Trevor out of trouble. Keep him with beautiful exotic women. The very girls that Mischa had made friends with upon her arrival.

Orenda also had other duties to perform, and Trevor could not know about such things, yet. Their Thane, who was their father wanted his son left in the dark as a precaution.

So, on the first day of school. Orenda sat with her brother with a smirk. He would be too busy with school and the girls to notice her absence all that often. It was for the better!

First Day of School!

Welcome students to your first day!
-*Ambassador Tina*

It was a warm sunny day with a cool breeze that was gentle and soothing. The students gathered and went to their assigned classes. It was an exciting day for everyone. This was something new and different.

Today, Glen and Neola walked with Princess Catrice and Gianna. They talked and got along. The princess thought it weird that they all acted like nothing happened. Maybe it was for the better.

They reached their class. And went to the front desks. The half-circled room rose in the aisles with seats and desks. Students were filling the seats. Glen sat at the front row on one end with Neola beside him then Catrice and Gianna next. They made sure to sit together and this would be their desks for the year.

Trevor came in and sat behind Glen along with the girls he had met. Quorra sat beside Trevor then Umay and Mischa, with Orenda who was barely noticed.

Violet and Poppy came in and sat at the top row on the exact opposite side of the room at the far end.

Rose and her guardian went to the top row center. Seemed she wanted to observe everything from there.

Further away from the front row was two pools of water. One salt and the other fresh. There they were connected to the river and the ocean. Here the aquatic creature would do there schooling. There were some that could be on land for long periods of time, even live on land for years before going back into the water. The choice was left to them where they wanted to sit.

Mermaids liked to sit on rocks with their tails in the water and there was a set up for just that.

Kelpie had to stay in the water but could have their upper bodies out.

There were so many water type creatures, that the pools were full.

In the center of it all stood Doctor Taka and Ambassador Tina. They were almost late coming into school because of Tina's nagging desire for a one last go of loving making. Taka smiled at the event. It did help settle their nervousness at any rate.

The two women observed all the students. How they entered the class. Where they sat. How they acted and interacted. Everyone thus far was on their best behavior. The Ambassador and Doctor were impressed.

Everyone began to quiet down. When it became silent in the room. The ambassador spoke.

"Welcome students to your first year of schooling. We hope this experience will greatly improve your outlook on life and have a grand old time in the process." Tina's voice was strong and loud enough for everyone to hear. As it should be with the acoustics in the room.

"This is the first class that I have welcomed thus far and throughout the day I shall welcome the rest of the students in the school. I hope you know your schedules and the rules. I hope your stay here in our fair nation will be pleasant. Thank you, students, and have a great first day," she finished and bowed.

The students applauded her and brought a smile to her face.

Tina then left the classroom and Taka took center stage. She wore her glasses and her uniform. The same one they all had first met her in. She held a pointer stick in her hand.

"As some of you may know, my name is Doctor Taka. You may call me Professor Taka if you like, but Doctor is fine," she said.

"Today you shall get books filled with blank parchment inside. These will be your workbooks you shall write in. I shall also explain the work curriculum," she paused to let everyone absorb her words.

"Today will be more of an explanation day. There will be no work until tomorrow. Today is to get you settled into a routine of how the process of this school, works. So, bare with me. All this is a work in progress and things may change along the way to make things easier for all. Not to mention better organization." Again, Taka stopped and watched who listened and who did not. So far everyone was paying close attention.

"All your time will not consist to being in this classroom. There will be activities for everyone. A kind of sport events that you will be able to join. There will be daily exercises and even trips to other places," she revealed.

There were some commotions and talk about this. They were finding interest. This was a good sign.

"There will be breaks in between classes for you get to your next class or event. Depending on what you chose to do in the next few days. You will have a lunch period where you have free time to interact with one another and eat your food. There will be clubs you can join for after classes here at the school," Taka said. Her voice reached everyone in the room. There was excitement at these prospects. Taka liked this.

She watched everyone and how they reacted to her words. Most were interested. Although there were a few who were skeptical. Violet watched like some sort of predator. Not only did she watch the teacher, but Glen and his friends. Trevor and his girls. Of course, she eyed her sister Rose like some sort of plague that had to be eradicated.

Taka dreaded that there would be some troubles, in the near, future with those two girls.

Then the doors to the class burst open and a girl and her guardian trotted in like they owned the place.

Taka let out an exasperated breath. Speaking of trouble. She just walked in. She was warned this bitch would eventually show up. Taka just wished that it would not have been today.

"Hello, everyone! My name is Talitha, Demon Princess," she said loudly and raised her hands in the air.

The demoness displayed her bikini body. She showed her curves. Her ass was bare even though she was covered in the front. Her top was so small that it only covered the nipples of her large breasts. Her dark pink skin was smooth with red glyph birthmarks all over her body. She had hooved feet with fiery tuffs of fur. Her clawed hands looked deadly and ready to rend. Her lush curvy mouth bore serrated teeth. Her crown of horns was large and displayed her power. Her yellow eyes gazed around in mirth.

"Take a seat and please do be quiet," Taka said. "I will not have any interruptions while students are trying to learn," Taka finished with a finality to her tone.

The demoness narrowed her eyes and pouted her lips.

"You are no fun," she muttered under her breath and found a seat, along with her guardian who remained cloaked.

Taka did not like that Talitha was here. She was too unpredictable and dangerous. Demons had a bad habit of causing chaotic situations. Right now, the demoness sat with a bored expression and pouted. Not a good sign until she eyed Glen. Then she perked up with interest.

Fuck, Taka thought. Glen's presence was cause for trouble.

A clawed nail went in between the demoness' teeth, and she had this nasty grin upon her devilish features.

Damnit!

Already problems were about to start in this school year. Taka tried to put it from her mind for the time being.

"Now, we shall take a roll call of names and I would like you to introduce yourself and tell us a little bit about who you are. Thank You," Taka explained. She called out the first name.

School was now in session!

**Continued in
Chimera's Lay
Book 2
Jade Lamia**

Made in the USA
Middletown, DE
31 May 2021